MIST ACROSS THE MOORS

When Tracy spent a night with Brett Hardwick
on the moors, it was due to force of circumstances and couldn't have been more innocent,
but unfortunately the episode led to a lot of
damaging gossip. So Tracy suggested to her
friend Wayne Eastwood that they should
become 'engaged' to put a stop to it. It was a
suggestion that was to create more problems
than it solved . . .

MIST ACROSS THE MOORS

BY

LILIAN PEAKE

MILLS & BOON LIMITED
17-19 FOLEY STREET
LONDON W1A 1DR

First published 1972

This edition 1972

© *Lilian Peake 1972*

ISBN 0 263 71321 0

Made and Printed in Great Britain by C. Nicholls & Company Ltd., The Philips Park Press, Manchester.

CHAPTER I

I GRIPPED the steering wheel and wished there was radar in the minibus to help me penetrate the obliterating blanket of moorland mist.

"Mist?" I thought angrily. "Is that what they call it in these parts? This is the thickest *fog* I've ever seen."

I must have spoken aloud, because the man at my side answered, "Misnomer or not, Miss Johns, we've got to get through it somehow, so if you're frightened, it will be better for us all if you hand over the driving to me."

I shook my head. "No, it's quite all right, Mr. Hardwick. You've got to rest your leg. You've driven for some miles to-day, and . . ."

"Miss Johns," Mr. Hardwick said, slowly and clearly, "this is the third time I have asked you to let me take over. Now," he raised his voice, "I absolutely insist that you do so."

I gripped the steering wheel harder and gritted my teeth. The man was putting me off. If he would just be quiet and let me get on with it. . . .

"Miss Johns," his hard voice came again, "as your superior, as the acting headmaster of the school you teach in, I *order* you to let me drive."

Just how nasty could he get? His hand came down on to the steering wheel. I reacted swiftly, regardless of the consequences, and tried to wrench the steering wheel from his grasp. The vehicle swerved out of control to the left, the dozen boys in the back yelled and screeched as they sprawled on top of each other, and the minibus slithered sideways on to the rutted, sloping verge, coming to rest at an alarming angle.

"Good God," muttered Mr. Hardwick, as he pushed away strands of my long brown hair from his mouth and neck. I had fallen on top of him and he seemed to be having some difficulty in disentangling his body from mine. "Heaven preserve me from women drivers after this!"

In the heat of the moment, I quite forgot the respect I should be showing my superior. "How can you say that?" I cried, jerking myself upright and free of him with some difficulty, against the drunken slope of the vehicle. "It was *your* fault, not mine. You tried to take control of the steering wheel. Don't you know you should never, never do that?"

It was perhaps lucky for me that the boys' squeals and scuffles behind us distracted my superior's attention from my disrespectful remarks.

"We must see to the boys," he rapped out. "I can't get out this side, the door's sticking, so you'll have to heave yourself up and get out your side. Go on, I'll give you a hand."

So I edged myself upwards towards the door, forced it open and with my feet pushing against the upholstery and the propelling motion of the acting headmaster's hands against my seat, I scrambled free. I had no time to assess the situation we were in because an argument had broken out amongst the boys and it was threatening to erupt into a first-class fight. I rushed round to the side and, because the slant of the minibus had almost put the door handle out of my reach, I had to stand on my toes and stretch upwards to grip it. I opened the door and pushed my head inside.

"Shut up, you lot!" I yelled, hoping my superior wouldn't reprimand me for my unladylike words. "Can't you see we're in trouble?"

I might have been cooing to a baby for all the notice they took of me. Two strong hands gripped my waist and lifted me aside, a tall, dark-haired man thrust his thunderous face into the vehicle and shouted, "If you little devils don't stop your nonsense at once, I'll give good hidings to the lot of you!"

The effect was remarkable. The noise level subsided so fast the silence that followed became unnerving, and all that was left was the strangled breathing of the dozen pupils of King Henry's School for Boys.

"Right, now perhaps we can have a bit of peace and quiet. First, get yourselves out of this bus, one by one, in an orderly fashion. No fights, no kicking, no sly digs in the ribs. If there's any more nonsense, I personally will administer the necessary punishment, corporal or otherwise, when we do finally get out of this mess." He turned away and muttered under his breath, "If we ever do."

I watched the boys, unkempt and wild-eyed with fright, propel themselves upwards against the slope of the minibus, jump out one by one, and stare around uncertainly.

"How did it happen, sir?" one of them wanted to know.

"Ask her," growled the acting headmaster. "*I* wasn't driving."

"My dad always says you can't trust women drivers," said a boy with red hair.

Mr. Hardwick allowed himself a passing smile. "Then your father and I now have something in common, Miller."

"Shut up, *Rufus*," I hissed, breaking all the rules and calling the boy by the nickname he despised.

"Miss Johns," the acting headmaster's cutting tones reduced me to size, "remember your position — unless of course I'm mistaken and you are a contemporary of the boy, and not his teacher."

I gave him a filthy look for making me feel thirteen, but he smiled in a superior way and turned his back on me.

"What do we do now, Dad?"

Mr. Hardwick walked across to his son, who stood forlorn and shivering in the background. "We'll have to get out of this mess, won't we, lad?"

I was shaken by the tenderness in his voice as he spoke to his son. I was surprised that such a hard, unyielding man

7

could be so gentle. I could see he was trying to disguise his anxiety and as he moved away from the boys, I followed timidly. I thought I might get my head snapped off, but I asked him, "What – what do you intend to do, Mr. Hardwick? I'm very sorry for what happened."

He shrugged. "All right, forget it. I didn't exactly help by what I did." He looked at me then. "I'm sorry, too."

I felt the apology must have cost him some effort. He didn't seem the sort of man who apologised often. He looked at his watch.

"We're late already. Nearly twenty miles before we reach the youth hostel. In this soup," he looked disgustedly at the mist which blanketed the landscape, "that means nearly two hours' driving."

I sensed his indecision and, steeling myself to his certain irritation at my daring to interfere, I suggested, "Before we think about what we're going to do, wouldn't it be better to try to right the minibus, Mr. Hardwick?"

He didn't growl, he smiled, and it was such a pleasant smile my pulse did curious things. "You have something there, Miss Johns. You could be right."

I didn't wait to be told, I went into action. "Come on, boys, we'll all push."

There was a mad rush to the rear of the vehicle, and the bedraggled schoolboys turned into little demons and started to fight and kick to get the best place to put their hands and push.

"Miss Johns," a weary voice wafted over the waving heads, "if you had only thought before you acted, you would have realised that we can't all push. In the first place, there isn't room. Secondly, someone's got to pull." He climbed into the bus through the side door and found a length of rope under a seat. He came out backwards and uncoiled the rope. He tied it securely in two places to the front bumper. "Now, I want five boys with me here. The rest of you can push, except

8

Miss Johns. She's a light-weight, so she can sit in the bus and steer." He seemed to mutter something under his breath and the boys with him laughed.

"He's just said 'heaven help us', Miss Johns," Rufus called spitefully, then everybody laughed, except me, and I clenched my fists. I scrambled upwards into the minibus and had to brace myself against the slope to the left. I felt scared as I pressed the starter and the engine roared into life.

"For pity's sake don't mow the boys down, Miss Johns. However murderous you may feel towards me, at least spare them."

I clenched my teeth as well as my fists at that crack.

"Hand-brake off, Miss Johns, foot down, Miss Johns. . . . Now, everybody heave. . . ."

Fifteen minutes later the minibus was parked, decorous and sober, on a piece of level ground at the roadside. Mr. Hardwick gazed around and was human enough to be shivering. "This filthy mist, it gets everywhere. The cold's seeping into my bones and I'm hungry."

He flapped his hands at the 'so am I, sirs' and looked at me. "Food, Miss Johns? I take it we've some reserves tucked away?"

"Yes, Mr. Hardwick. We've got some sandwiches left from lunch, and there are a couple of sliced loaves, butter and cheese somewhere. We could boil a kettle on the Primus stove and make some tea. . . ."

"Good." Mr. Hardwick waved his arm. "Get down to your sandwiches, boys. Miss Johns, see that they get back into the bus in an orderly fashion."

I put on my best sergeant-major manner and fixed them with a menacing stare. One or two started to give trouble, but I grabbed their collars and shook them. Colin Hardwick was the last to get in, and someone tried to push him out again. I went to his aid, feeling for some reason a soft spot for this sensitive son of the stern-faced acting head. I dug deep into

9

Colin's haversack, found his sandwiches and gave them to him. "All right?" I asked, smiling at him, and he nodded.

Mr. Hardwick was sitting in the driver's seat. I sat beside him and raked in my haversack for food.

"Don't 'baby' my son, Miss Johns," Mr. Hardwick said to the windscreen. "He's thirteen, the same as the others. He should be able to look after himself just as well."

"I'm sorry." I couldn't think why, but his reprimand upset me, and I ate my sandwiches in silence. Mr. Hardwick was as quiet as I was. Now and then he looked round at the mist disgustedly, then lapsed into a mindless stare. I wished desperately that we could find something in common to talk about, but all we did was listen to the chatter behind us and chewed instead of talked. We finished eating and he crumpled his sandwich paper. "Got a place for rubbish?"

I found a large paper bag and held it out. He dropped the rubbish in. "Better see that the boys do likewise. Mustn't leave our litter behind us. Then what about that tea?"

I knew I had to obey his orders – I was, after all, a very junior member of the teaching staff – but my annoyance at being treated like a servant must have penetrated his thick skin, because he said, with a hint of apology, "My leg is aching. So if you don't mind. . . ."

"I'm sorry, I forgot about your leg. Did you strain it when you were pulling on that rope?"

"Yes."

I jumped out and got the Primus stove going with the boys' help. I filled the kettle from one of the water bottles and made some tea in a giant-sized teapot we had brought with us. Our tempers improved noticeably as our appetites were satisfied, and even Mr. Hardwick became more approachable. He sat with the boys and talked to them, and I decided to wander off on my own. Mr. Hardwick's voice followed me into the mist.

"Don't go too far away, Miss Johns."

10

I shivered and wished my slacks didn't cling so clammily to my legs, or my hair hang so hopelessly in long damp tails round my neck. I put up the hood of my wind-cheater and gazed at the mist which filled my nostrils with a steamy smell and formed stinging drops on my eyelashes. I knew the landscape must be beautiful somewhere behind that grey curtain, and wished the geography field trip could have gone on as planned, but it seemed unlikely now.

We'd made arrangements for the trip at the start of last term, while Mr. Hardwick was still head of the geography department. Then the headmaster had been taken ill and forced to retire. Because Mr. Hardwick was deputy head, he had temporarily taken Mr. Browning's place.

I turned and went back. The worried frown on Mr. Hardwick's face eased away when he saw me. The ordnance survey map was spread across the bonnet and he was studying it with the boys grouped round him.

"We must be nearly two thousand feet up, sir," one of them said.

"Crossfell's nearly three thousand feet," Jackson boasted, as if the mountain was his property. He pointed vaguely to the north. "It's in that direction."

"You're a sap, Jackson," Colin snorted. "You've got no sense of direction. It's there." He raised his arm and swung it to the north-west.

Warding off the threatened argument, Mr. Hardwick folded the map carefully and slipped it into his pocket. "Right," he said shortly. "I've decided. We go home, as soon as weather conditions permit."

He ignored all the protests and groans. "I'm responsible, with Miss Johns here, for your safety, and I'm taking no chances. In the circumstances, it would be madness to go on." He turned to me. "Miss Johns, see them into the bus."

I didn't obey at once. I dared to question his judgment. "Is it wise, Mr. Hardwick, to drive in this? I mean," I hesitated

11

when I saw the thunder in his eyes, "we came up some very steep hills on the way and there were some nasty bends, and in this bad visibility. . . ." I tailed off, quelled to silence by the look in his eye.

"Since *I* shall be driving, Miss Johns," he said, over-politely, "we need not worry too much, need we?"

"But – but what about your leg?"

"Damn my leg." His tone brought an end to our one-sided discussion. "Settle those boys down. When you've done that, stand outside and help me turn the bus round." Did he need to talk to me so sharply in front of the boys? "It could be a dangerous manoeuvre in this mist, but I doubt if there'll be another driver mad enough to come this way for hours."

So we began our hazardous journey back. It grew dark and the mist stopped dithering about and turned decisively into fog, thick impenetrable fog. Visibility worsened and Mr. Hardwick began to show that even his nerves were not made of toughened steel.

Without warning, he steered the minibus off the narrow, moorland road and pulled up in a lay-by which had been cut into overhanging rock. The cliff-face gave some protection. He turned and looked at me.

"I'm afraid this is it, Miss Johns. We'll have to spend the night here and hope that by morning things have improved. I don't know about you, but," he peered into the blackness, "I simply haven't got the nerve to drive in these conditions."

"But, Mr. Hardwick – stay here for the night?"

He smiled and lowered his voice. "Don't look so shattered. There's nothing improper about it. I admit the proportion of males to female is a little on the high side, but –" he shrugged, "we all have sleeping bags, I take it?" I nodded. "The boys can curl up where they are, and you and I will have to relax somehow in the front here. We should manage to get some sleep." He opened the door. "Come on, let's supervise their bedtime."

12

It was over an hour before the mass of writhing young bodies was still, and another hour before the jokes and whispers stopped, and steady breathing took their place.

I wriggled into my sleeping-bag and half sat, half lay on the seat. But it was no good. I couldn't sleep, somehow I couldn't slide into sweet oblivion. I tried all the tricks I knew – counted sheep, went through the alphabet forwards and backwards, counted numbers till my brain felt like a roundabout. When I reached a thousand, I started to panic.

I turned my head and peered in the darkness at the man beside me. Was he asleep? He was incredibly still. I studied what I could see of his handsome profile and felt a stirring of feeling inside me which increased my panic. I began to fidget, I began to perspire. I felt suffocated in the restricting narrowness of the sleeping bag and the wall of fog outside.

"What's the matter?" Mr. Hardwick turned his head. "Can't you sleep?"

I shook my head. "I've tried everything, but –"

I think he smiled. "You're not the only one. Nor can I."

We looked at each other and I could just make out in the gloom how thick his eyebrows were and how they almost met across the bridge of his nose. I was sure that those eyes which were usually so austere and cold were smiling now.

"What shall we do about it, Miss Johns?"

"I don't know. I just don't know."

He raised his hand and felt inside his sleeping bag. "Somewhere in here, I have a shoulder. Would you care to try it for size?"

"Oh, no, thanks, Mr. Hardwick. I couldn't. . . ."

"Couldn't you? Why not? Too many barriers between us – status, position and all that? But good heavens, in the circumstances –" he moved his arm towards me, but I shrank away.

"All right," he sounded hurt, "we'll just have to pass the time talking, won't we? What shall we talk about?"

13

That was another problem. Then I asked, "How – how did you hurt your leg?"

"Ah yes, as good an opening gambit as any. I damaged a muscle playing football too enthusiastically in the garden with my son. But don't tell anyone, will you? It sounds so unromantic."

I felt a little bolder. "You play football?"

"Occasionally. Why the surprise?"

"It doesn't go with your – your image, somehow."

He laughed. "You don't think I'm human enough, is that it?"

"Yes."

"You'd be surprised how human I am, Miss Johns."

He was silent after that. I panicked. How could I make him talk again? Somehow I had to stop him sleeping and leaving me awake for the long hours of the night, so I asked, "Did your wife mind you bringing your son away this weekend?"

His head shot round. "My wife? My wife died ten years ago."

For some reason, my heartbeats increased in speed alarmingly. "But at school, they told me you've got someone called Elaine. I thought she was your wife."

"Ah, Elaine. She's my housekeeper, latest in a succession of them. But she'll stay. Elaine's just a little different from the others. She's special. She's really an old friend of my sister's. She's a widow with a young son. She was in need of a job, and I wanted a housekeeper, so it all worked out very well. She's been with me roughly two years."

My heartbeats slowed down. So it was like that, was it? I did a sum in my head, then said, "So your boy was very young when his mother died?"

"Very young. It's a time I don't even like to think about, let alone talk about."

"I'm sorry."

14

The mist moved in mysterious patterns outside the windows. The stillness was intense and unnerving. The desire in me for warmth, for contact with another human being, became overwhelming. I moved restlessly and started shivering.

"Miss Johns, there's no need to sit there quivering like a leaf. My offer is still open." Mr. Hardwick patted his shoulder. "It's well-upholstered, so come on, try it."

His arm lifted out of the top of the sleeping bag and stretched out behind me. He pulled me towards him. This time, it didn't even occur to me to resist. I shuffled along the seat and rested my head against him. His fingers gripped me through the quilting of my sleeping bag and we were still. "Comfortable, Miss Johns?" he asked softly, above my head.

"Just right, thank you, Mr. Hardwick." I sighed and relaxed my whole body. The shaking stopped. Somehow it seemed to be the most natural thing in the world to be where I was.

"Mr. Hardwick?" My small voice crept up to him. "Do you think you'll be the next headmaster?"

He laughed shortly. "I doubt it very much. The interview for the job is this coming Tuesday, did you know? I'm on the short list, but they probably only put me on it out of courtesy."

"But you are the acting head, and already doing the job."

"That makes no difference. The number of times appointments committees have gone over the heads of people like me who are acting this or that would fill a volume. Anyway, the old fuddy-duddies who sit on the committee will probably consider me too young for the job." I looked up at him questioningly. "If you must know, Miss Johns, I'm thirty-seven. Old to you, perhaps, at your tender age. . . ."

I shook my head violently. "I'm twenty-three, you know."

"Oh, very old and wise," he said with a smile in his voice. "Secondly, I'm too well known to the powers-that-be as one who wants to change the existing order of things. In local government, someone like me is anathema to all the old traditionalists who still haunt our county halls and council

15

offices. So my chances of getting the headship are very small indeed."

"It would be so nice if you did get it, Mr. Hardwick."

He squeezed my arm gently. "Thank you for that."

"If they did appoint you, would you make a lot of changes?"

He thought carefully. "I'd certainly want to make changes, but how many I might actually achieve would remain to be seen."

I persisted, "The changes I mean are things like the compulsory wearing of academic gowns during school hours that Mr. Browning insisted on. I think it's out of date and it's embarrassing, too."

He laughed. "Embarrassing? That's an odd word to apply to things as voluminous as gowns. They seem to me to be as sexless and – well, neuter, a garment as anything I've come across."

I laughed, too. "I don't mean it in that sense. I mean financially embarrassing. I bought my gown second-hand – although even that's not correct – I got it in a sale from a clothing-hire firm, and it was torn in a few places. I mended it, but the tears are coming back. The fabric's in shreds and it's only the folds of the material that hide the fact." I sighed. "I suppose I'll just have to scrape up enough money for another one, soon."

There was a short silence, and he said, "I think we're getting too serious, don't you? Let's change the subject."

"All right." I looked up at him, and taking advantage of our closeness asked, "Are you going to marry your housekeeper, Mr. Hardwick?"

He gave my shoulder a little shake. "My private life, Miss Johns, is none of your business."

I drew away from him slightly. "I'm sorry." He pulled me back.

"Don't be silly, Miss Johns."

I closed my eyes and relaxed again. There was a movement

16

behind and a groping arm crept between us. I smothered a scream.

We pulled apart quickly and as I became separated from the man beside me, I felt an unbearable pain as though part of me had been wrenched away.

Colin's quavering voice broke in, "I'm sorry I frightened you, Miss Johns, but I want to go outside. Dad, could you come with me? I'm scared to go alone."

"Of course, son." He disentangled himself from me, pulled off his sleeping bag, slipped on his shoes and helped Colin outside. They went into the gloom. A strange loneliness was everywhere. I became convinced they were lost in the darkness. I panicked again, and wondered if I should wake the others and start searching. It seemed hours since they had gone.

It was in fact only a few minutes later that their shapes formed into recognisable figures and they climbed back into the minibus. Mr. Hardwick settled his son into his sleeping bag, managing to do so without waking the others. Then he took off his shoes, pulled his bag over his legs and upwards to his shoulders.

I had slumped away from him into the corner. He reached across for me, and I felt him unzip my sleeping bag until it was low enough for him to get his arm in.

"You don't mind, do you?" he whispered. "My arm wasn't very happy outside."

I shook my head. By now I had temporarily lost the power of speech. He drew my head down to his shoulder and I nestled close against him as if that was where I really belonged. Somewhere, I was sure, the moon was shining in a clear, star-bright sky and I could swear I heard a nightingale nearby. But when I opened my eyes, I saw through the windows the drifting fog and heard the deathly silence.

"Tracy?" I looked up, startled. "That is your name, isn't it? In the circumstances, Tracy, I think we should dispense

17

with formalities. For what it's worth, my name is Brett. Say it."

I grew bold, rolled it round and round my tongue drunkenly. "Brett, Brett. M'm, it's a nice name and I like it. Brett, Brett. . . ."

I was sure he was smiling. "Tracy," he said, "where do you live?"

I told him. "It's a long way from the school, but it was the best available at the price I could pay. It's a large old house, divided into bed-sitters. I cook on a gas-ring, share a bathroom with five other tenants. You never see the landlady except when you want to make a complaint, and that doesn't do much good." I lifted my head. "I could never invite someone like you there."

"And why not?"

"It's not good enough."

His hand caressed my arm as though trying to rub away a hurt. "Never mind, you'll probably be getting married before long, won't you?"

I laughed. "First catch your boy-friend."

"But I thought you had one. What about Eastwood, the other geography teacher?"

"Wayne? Oh, I go out with him sometimes, but that's all. We're not serious."

"He doesn't exactly strike me as a one-girl man."

"No, he's not.

There was a warm silence, and I could hear the steady pounding of his heart beneath my ear. "Brett, how long were you actually married, before your wife died?"

The pounding increased alarmingly and I peered up at him, wondering why. "Five years. We hadn't been living in – perfect harmony, to put it mildly, for some time before that." He looked down and I felt his breath on my face, so close to his. "But you've no right to be asking these personal questions, young woman."

18

I coloured in the darkness and was glad he couldn't see me properly. "I'm very sorry, Brett."

He squeezed my arm reassuringly.

"Anyway," I shifted a little in his arms, "I don't think I'll ever marry, after what happened between my parents."

"Tell me what happened, Tracy."

His breath was stirring strands of my hair, and I rubbed my cheek against the wool of his high-necked pullover. I must have felt like a kitten seeking comfort and caresses. He responded by tightening his hold on me. "They quarrelled with one another incessantly right through my childhood and only stayed together, as they said, for my sake. They stuck it until I left home and went to University. Then they parted, and now they're divorced."

"Do you ever see them?"

"My father, never. He's married again, so has my mother. They've both got stepchildren. I see my mother sometimes."

"So you're virtually on your own?"

I nodded against him. His arms held me more securely, and his body became a refuge and I sighed with pure contentment.

He whispered, "Try to sleep now, Tracy."

"Yes, Brett. Good night, Brett."

I drifted off at last and later on, in my sleep, I'm sure I murmured his name and rubbed my cheek against his chest. I think I started to wake, but felt a gentle pressure on my hair and went back to my dreams.

Someone was shaking me, but I didn't want to respond.

"Miss Johns, wake up. Dad says it's time we were getting something to eat." I stirred and my cheek felt for the softness and rhythmic breathing of a broad masculine chest, but I found instead the coldness of the leather upholstery. I was propped sideways against the side of the minibus and I was alone on the front seat.

19

I shook myself awake. "Sorry, Colin. Why didn't you wake me earlier?"

"Dad said not to disturb you."

"Good morning, Miss Johns." The brisk, impersonal voice acted like a cold shower. My head jerked round and I looked at the face at the driver's window. The mouth was smiling, but the grey eyes were somehow withdrawn.

"I'm sorry, Mr. Hardwick, but you should have called me before."

I struggled with the zip fastener on my sleeping bag. It had become caught in the folds of the material, and I turned pink in my efforts to free it. The door opened and two hands stretched across and took over the operation.

"Sleep well, Miss Johns?" Our eyes locked for a shock-filled moment, and my blood started on a mad relay race through my veins. The zip gave suddenly and the moment was gone.

"Yes, thank you, Mr. Hardwick," I answered sedately, and lowered my eyes.

I was left alone and searched in my handbag for comb and compact. I longed for a wash. I pushed the things back into my bag and scrambled out. I asked one of the boys, "Is there a stream anywhere?"

"Down there, Miss Johns. Follow me, I'll take you."

I got my flannel and towel from my haversack and went after him. Brett was down there, drying his face.

He smiled as I crouched beside the crystal-clear water and dabbled my flannel in it.

"It's ice-cold, Miss Johns, I'm warning you."

I trailed my fingers in it as it flowed and eddied over the stones, I washed myself and rubbed my cheeks dry. My face was glowing when I put my towel away and put on my make-up. I moved across to the driving seat and looked in the rear-view mirror. I combed my hair until it fluffed round my face, and I felt as though I was being watched. My eyes shifted a fraction to look behind my own image in the mirror, but there was no one there.

Brett came from the rear and pushed his head in the window. "Miss Johns, when you've finished putting icing on a cake which is perfectly good without it," he smiled, "could you find some food? We've a dozen starving boys to feed, and our lives won't be worth living until we do. On our way back, we can stop in a town and stock up again, if necessary."

His voice had become businesslike and I flushed guiltily at his tone.

"I'm sorry I'm taking so long, Mr. Hardwick." I put my things back into my handbag and scrambled out, just missing his feet. His arms came out instinctively to steady me.

"It's early in the morning to be drunk, Tracy." His eyes were smiling and I pulled away from him, embarrassed without the blanket of darkness to close the yawning gap of status between us.

"I'm sorry, Mr. Hardwick," I said again.

He was still smiling as he let me go. I looked round. The mist had almost gone and the coming of daylight had parted the curtains on the landscape. I had no time to take in the beauty of the moors and the sheep-speckled hills and valleys. I heard the bleating of the lambs and the clear, thrilling call of the curlews as I went into the side door of the minibus. I raked in the box which contained the stores and found the last of the bread, a carton of milk and one or two bottles of lemonade.

The boys straggled back from the stream and nearby slopes, their voices carrying across the wide moorland silence. Colin and Jackson were still arguing about Crossfell. Colin appealed to his father, who lined up the map and told them exactly which summit it was. "It's the highest peak in the Pennines," he told them.

"Must we still go back, sir?" Jackson asked.

"Yes. We've lost too much time, I'm afraid. We would have

21

returned home tomorrow, anyway. Looking back on it, Miss Johns, this trip was too short. Next time we plan a field trip, we shall have to allow more time."

"Yes, Mr. Hardwick." I turned to the others. "Never mind, boys, you'll have tomorrow to recover at home before the summer term starts on Tuesday."

A dozen groans oozed from a dozen youthful throats and everyone laughed. An hour later we were on our way home. I was glad Brett was driving. After ditching the vehicle yesterday, I felt very nervous of driving again on these unpredictable moorland roads.

"How's your leg, Mr. Hardwick? I'm afraid I forgot to ask."

He glanced at me briefly. "Much better, thanks. I'd forgotten about it, too."

He obviously didn't want to talk. He seemed preoccupied, concentrating on the bends and steep hills, alert all the while for straying sheep and lambs. Some time later he slackened speed.

"Will you take over, Miss Johns? I feel like a rest."

I tensed. "Well, I will if you want me to, Mr. Hardwick, but after what happened yesterday, do you trust me to drive?"

"Trust you? Of course I trust you, absolutely."

As I moved into the driving seat, I laughed. "That's more than I do. If you knew me as well as I know me, you wouldn't say that!"

He didn't laugh with me. He turned his head away. "I don't trust many women nowadays, Tracy, but I think I'd make an exception of you."

"Thanks for your confidence in me, Mr. Hardwick." I laughed again. "I hope I never do anything to – to betray that trust."

"So do I," was all he said.

I soon got over my nervousness, and we alternated with the driving all the way back to Nottinghamshire. We delivered the boys to their homes, and then only Colin was left, waiting impatiently for his father to give me back my hand.

"Good-bye, Tracy," Brett said. "It's been a useful and – interesting trip."

"Even though it didn't yield any results?"

He smiled. "That's a matter of opinion."

My hand was growing warm in his. "Good-bye, Mr. Hardwick." I added shyly, "Good luck at the interview on Tuesday." And because I knew it would be for the last time, I dared to whisper, "Good-bye, Brett."

CHAPTER II

I WAS racing along the corridor to the staff room, my gown ballooning out behind me. Those unwritten notes were on my mind, those pages of notes I'd meant to prepare during the Easter holidays, but somehow there had never been time.

"Miss Johns!" The voice thundered after me and I came to a crash stop. My gown caught me up and wrapped itself around me like a great black strait-jacket. I turned round to see Brett Hardwick standing half in, half out of a classroom door. "Will you come back here, please?"

I walked back to him, more sedately this time. "Yes, Mr. Hardwick?"

He glowered. "Surely you're aware of the rule that prohibits running in the corridor? How can we enforce it amongst the boys, if the staff don't observe it?"

"I'm sorry, Mr. Hardwick. I was in a hurry."

"That was only too obvious." I looked into his face, and frowned. What was the matter with him? Then I remembered, perhaps he was on edge because of the interview this afternoon.

His next words knocked everything else from my mind. "Where's Mr. Eastwood?"

I began to walk a tightrope. I knew where Mr. Eastwood was — travelling back from a holiday with some friends on the south coast.

"Don't tell His Nibs," he'd said on the last day of term, "but I may be absent without leave on the first morning back. Be a pet, Tracy, and cover up for me. Give my class some work and keep them quiet. Don't let me down."

I took a deep breath and forgot to let it out. I had let him down.

"I can see you know. Where is he?"

"He – I don't – he just isn't in, Mr. Hardwick. I don't know where he could be." And that, I thought, is the truth. How do I know which part of which motorway he's on at this moment? "Perhaps he's ill. . . ." My voice trailed away.

The acting headmaster looked at me narrowly, then permitted himself a half-smile. "All right, Miss Johns. We'll leave it at that, but next time you cover up for him, do it more convincingly. I'm an old hand at it myself, remind me to give you some lessons." I smiled back, but his good humour didn't last. "As soon as he arrives, tell him I want to see him. Now, have you a class?"

"No, Mr. Hardwick. As a matter of fact," I went on chattily, "I was rushing to catch up with my note-making. I've got behind during the Easter holidays. . . ."

"Well," the headmaster wasn't in a chatty mood, "you've got a class now. You'll have to leave your notes and do some teaching, since your friend is taking extended leave of absence, without permission." He turned into the classroom and I followed. "They were making one hell of a row as I came past. After the talking-to I've given them, I don't think they'll give you much trouble. Now this is where they tell me they've got to." He gave me full instructions and left me. For the next hour, I chided myself for my forgetfulness.

Just before two o'clock, Wayne Eastwood wandered into the staff room. I was leaving to take my next class and I was late. He seized me round the waist and my folders went flying across the room.

Wayne made a growling noise and pulled me against him. "I'm hungry for you, pet." He tried to kiss me. "Missed me?"

"No. Should I have? Anyway, I must go. I – er – had to do a cover-up job for a Mr. Eastwood this morning. I – I forgot about your class, Wayne. I'm sorry. Mr. Hardwick found them

25

without a teacher and he wants to see you. Now."

"The devil he does! Who does he think he is? He's only the acting head. He can wait. I've got a class. Remind me to spank you later for getting me into hot water."

I picked up my folders. "The interview for the headship's this afternoon, Wayne, did you know? Mr. Hardwick said he doesn't think he'll get it.

"Did he now, my pet? And when did he pour that little titbit into your pretty ear?"

"I – he – we had to stay the night on the moors and we –" I foundered, "Oh, I just heard it," I called over my shoulder, and raced to my class.

I made myself wait until four-thirty, then I had to know. I tapped timidly on the acting headmaster's door and opened it when he called "Come in".

There was something else besides surprise in his expression when he saw me, but it was gone at once. "Yes, Miss Johns?"

"I hope you don't mind my asking, Mr. Hardwick, but did you – did you get the headship?"

"Yes, I got it. You're the first to know."

"That's wonderful! I'm so glad. For your sake and the school's. And – and the staff's. Congratulations, Mr. Hardwick."

He thanked me and fiddled with his papers.

"Now you'll be able to make the changes you want, won't you?"

"Will I? I really don't know. I'm not thinking straight at the moment."

Will you celebrate this evening?"

His head came up. "Celebrate?" Then he shrugged. "No. That would imply that I'm carried away with delight, and that is something I never allow myself to be these days." He became brisk, and stood up. "But thank you for your interest, Miss Johns."

I knew I was being dismissed, but I lingered for a moment,

hoping to break through his barriers. The cool, questioning look that came my way sent me out of his study fast.

Wayne was in the staff room. He was in his usual seat and his feet decorated the table. He was smoking and watching the smoke rings rise to the ceiling. He looked at me. "Well, communicate. I can see you've got some news."

"We've got our new head, Wayne." I stopped, wondering how he would take it.

"Well, come on, give." He stubbed out his cigarette, lowered his feet and pulled me on to his knee. I tried to get away, but he held me down. "Not until you tell me."

"Mr. Hardwick got it."

"Did he now? So Hardwick's the golden boy? Hardly something to rejoice about, but anything will serve as an excuse for this." He pulled me down and kissed me. I was so preoccupied with my thoughts that I stayed where I was.

"He's going to make changes, Wayne. He told me so."

Wayne turned my face until I was looking at him. "What's this? Another of his little confidences? What else did he tell you, my pet? Whisper in my ear."

"I shouldn't if I were you, Miss Johns."

I struggled madly and got myself free of Wayne's arms. I stood, breathing hard, and faced the new headmaster, who was standing in the doorway watching us with stone-cold eyes.

"Eastwood, I've been waiting all day for you to give me an explanation of your absence this morning. I told Miss Johns to tell you," he turned a withering look in my direction and went on sarcastically, "but matters nearer to her heart must have made her forgetful. So I wish to see you now, Eastwood."

Wayne smiled indolently. "Beginning as you mean to go on, *Mr.* Hardwick?" He took out a cigarette and flicked his lighter. "I hear I have to congratulate you on your appointment." He put the flame to his cigarette and snapped the lighter shut. "Tracy here couldn't wait to tell me the news." He looked at me through the smoke and smiled. "We agreed that

27

whether it was good or bad was a matter of opinion, didn't we, pet?"

I turned on him. How could he let me down like that? "Wayne, what are you saying?" I turned to Brett. "It isn't true, Mr. Hardwick."

Brett ignored me. "I'm waiting, Eastwood."

I picked up my briefcase and ran out of the room.

"See you tonight, Tracy?" Wayne's words followed me along the corridor, but I shut my ears. He knew very well he wouldn't be seeing me tonight. If I didn't catch up with my work, I'd go under through lack of notes.

I drove home in my car, with its rattles and its rust, and parked in the driveway of the house I lived in. I went up the steps of the faded Victorian mansion and pushed open the front door. The oppressive smell of over-cooked vegetables hung around the dingy hall and I was thankful, as I went up stairs, that I had my own means of cooking food.

I toasted some bread on the only luxury I possessed – besides my car, although that was hardly a luxury – an electric toaster I'd bought out of my first month's salary eighteen months ago. I scrambled an egg in a saucepan on the gas-ring and spread the egg on the toast.

"Tracy, you in?" Dinah Rowe from the bed-sitter across the landing pushed her head round the door. "M'm, nice smell. Having toast with your tea?"

"Come in, Dinah." I lifted the tea-pot and raised my eyebrows.

"Please, love." Dinah sprawled in the armchair and reached out for the cup of tea. She was an art teacher at the local technical college, and her mode of dress labelled her strictly nonconformist. Her bright colours and low-cut necklines contrasted strongly with my conventional blouse and skirt. I made a mental note to brighten myself up, colour-wise.

"Well, how did the field trip go?"

"Ill-fated, Dinah. The weather was foul." I told her what

had happened. "Trust me to ditch the bus!"

"But you surely didn't have to manage all those kids alone?"

"Good heavens, no. Brett came with me. He was in charge."
My hand flew to my mouth.

"Brett?" Dinah crossed her elegant legs and offered me a
cigarette, but I shook my head. She was obviously going to
make the most of my mistake. "So it's Brett now, is it? How
come? Don't hold out on me. Tell Dinah your secrets. I swear
it'll go no further."

So I told her. She was, after all, my best friend. Dinah
stubbed out her cigarette. "Don't read too much into all that,
love. And above all, don't fall for the man. Rumour has it
he'll never re-marry after the last lot, and if he ever did, it
would be to that housekeeper of his."

"How do you know all this about him?"

"Matt Perry, the art teacher at your school, takes an evening
class at the technical college on the same night as me. He's
been at the school for years and knew Brett Hardwick's wife.
She was a teacher there, too. That's how she and Brett met,
it seems. They were in the same age group and the same department – geography."

I had to know. "What was she like, Dinah?"

"Cold, hard, bitchy, selfish and apparently very beautiful.
In fact, love, you couldn't be less like her if you tried."

"What happened between them? Did Matt tell you?"

"He said things went wrong from the start. And when the
baby started coming, she didn't want it, and told everyone
it was his fault. In the end she accused him openly of cruelty.
Matt told me how she died."

She stopped and stared at her foot, which she was twisting
round and round. I willed her to go on. "One day – he was
ill with 'flu at the time – she walked out on him. She'd booked
for a ski-ing holiday in the Alps and refused to cancel the
booking to look after him. She was out on the mountains one
morning when she – she was swept away by an avalanche."

29

I was shocked into silence. Then I asked, "Did he take it badly?"

"No one knows. He shut up like a clam. Apparently his sister came to his rescue and took the child for a while."

I frowned. "But how could she call Brett cruel? That's difficult to believe."

Dinah shrugged. "I don't know, he's a hard man, according to Matt. We were only discussing him because we wondered who would get the headmaster's job."

"He got it, Dinah, this afternoon."

Dinah sat up. "So he's made it? Good for him. He must have lived down the bad name his wife gave him. This must have been the councillors' way of saying 'all is forgiven'." She got up and stretched. "But take it from me, Tracy, he's not for you. Anyway, he's too old. He must be nearly forty."

"He's thirty-seven, Dinah. He told me."

"He told you, did he? Probably to warn you off, my dear." She wandered to the door. "See you some time."

There was a knock as she turned the handle. She opened the door and Wayne was standing outside. They stared at each other and the silence went on so long, it became embarrassing.

So I called out, "Wayne, what do you want?"

His eyes were still on Dinah when he came in. "That's a nice way to greet a man who's taken the trouble to come right across the town to see you!"

I thought it was about time I broke the spell and introduced them. Their hands touched, they smiled and moved in opposite directions. The door closed between them.

Wayne mopped his brow. "Now that was what I call an encounter with a capital E, brief but enchanting. Who's that devastating piece? Where have you been hiding her?"

"Nowhere. She's my neighbour." I changed the subject. "Why did you come, Wayne? I didn't think you meant it. I've got work to do, and it's urgent."

"To be honest, pet, I didn't intend to come, but after my interview with the new headmaster, I changed my mind." He looked pointedly at the teapot. "Any tea in there?"

"I might squeeze one more cup out of it." I did, and handed it to him. "Well, what happened?"

He sat in the armchair. "Oh, he ranted at me for being absent without leave – come to think of it, he's missed his vocation, he'd have done well in the army. He told me off for leaving you to cover up for me. He even raked up the past, and, as you know, I haven't always toed the line. But I gave back as good as I got, until –"

"But, Wayne, he's the headmaster now. You can't answer back like that. You might get into serious trouble."

"You didn't let me finish, sweetie. Until I remembered. Now he's been promoted, his job as head of the geography department's vacant, isn't it? So who's the most likely person to step into his shoes? Me, if I'm a good boy. So I changed my tune fast. It was 'yes, sir, no, sir' all the way to the door of the headmaster's study." He put down his empty cup and stood in front of me. "So my behaviour, Miss Johns, is going to be impeccable – at school." He pulled me up and kissed me. "This'll make you laugh, Tracy. He warned me off you."

I pulled away from him. "What right has he got to do that?"

"He said from what you told him, you had virtually no parents, and as your headmaster, he felt responsible for you, and was acting *in loco parentis*, as the Latin saying goes."

"And what exactly does that mean?"

"It means 'in place of parents', pet. In this case presumably, your father."

"My *father*?"

"Well, the man's getting on a bit, you know. He must be pushing forty, otherwise the old fogies on the interviewing committee wouldn't have appointed him."

"He's thirty-seven, he told me."

I could have kicked myself – I'd done it again. First I'd

31

told Dinah, now Wayne. He grabbed me. "Something else he told you, eh? The other night on the moors, I suppose. Was he taking a fatherly interest in you then? Tell me more."

I wriggled away from him. "He was being very kind and talked to me because I couldn't sleep. Nor could he. And – and he helped to keep me warm."

Wayne threw back his head and shouted with laughter. "Kind? No man is 'kind' to keep a girl like you warm. There's only one thing in a man's mind when he does that, sweetie-pie. And it's not kindness. You're a big girl now. You must know what I mean."

I turned scarlet. "Mr. Hardwick isn't like that."

Wayne grinned cynically. "Isn't he, my pet? Take it from me, I've worked with him, and I can tell you he's as normal in that respect as I am. And what's more, he's been married."

I pushed him away. "You're talking nonsense, of course. No one would be interested in me like that. I haven't got what it takes."

He grinned again. "No, sweetie?" He eyed me. "Don't fool yourself or underrate your charms." His fingers spanned my middle. "A neat, nipped-in waist, and all a man could ask for above and below. Extremely cuddly and a pretty face into the bargain. What more could a man desire? Any time you want the odd night out, just call on me, lady."

"Stop fooling, Wayne. I've got work to do."

When at last I managed to push him out of the door, he pointed to each one of the bed-sitters in turn. "Which one does that delectable creature live in? Come on, don't kept me in suspense."

I showed him. He pecked my cheek. "Thanks for telling me." He waved as he went down the stairs.

After Wayne's visit, I found it difficult to get down to work, but I was so desperate for teaching notes, I put Wayne's words to the back of my mind and started writing. It was late when I went to bed, but not so late that I didn't have time to think.

Brett's words drifted back. "You'd be surprised how human I am, Miss Johns," he'd said. I slept at last and dreamed that he was showing me just how human he could be.

A few days later I went to the staff room after lunch and found a group of teachers staring at the notice board.

"Two weeks as headmaster," Donald Basil, Latin and Greek teacher, was saying, "and he's throwing his weight about already."

"But surely, Donald, he won't stop us wearing them for assembly?" Mr. Simpson was the history master, and his voice remind me of the bleat of a sheep. "He doesn't mean us to abandon them altogether, surely?"

"My friends," intoned Wayne, grinning derisively on the edge of the group, "what will happen to the tone of the school if we lock our traditions away in the wardrobe with our academic cloaks of mourning? Stop the wearing of gowns? Tut tut, what is the world coming to?"

I thought it was time I knew what was going on. I pushed my way to the front and read aloud, "From Monday next, the wearing of academic gowns by the teaching staff will cease to be compulsory, and will be a matter of personal choice only. Gowns need not be worn at any time during school hours."

I clapped my hands. "I really must thank him. That was one of the things I asked him to change." Then I realised what I had said. So did the others. Every eye in the room fastened on to me.

"*You* asked him, Tracy?" Jenny Willis, teacher in the English department, said. "You mean to say he listens to someone as low down on the staff as you? In that case, I'm going to have a go at him myself about one or two things."

I realised then just how big my *faux pas* had been. "You can't do that, Jenny. This was a special occasion. I mean," I went on in confusion, as every eyebrow went up, "my suggestion this time happened to coincide with his ideas and fell on fertile ground."

"Well, anyway, Tracy, you did us a good turn. Now I can wear some nicer dresses for school instead of any old thing, as I have been doing because I knew it wouldn't show."

"I think it's scandalous. She's done me no good turn." Dr. Winsor, head of chemistry, looked at me with distaste.

"Too bad you won't be able to show off your Ph.D. trimmings at assembly any more, Doc," Wayne laughed, which made Dr. Winsor even more indignant.

Pete Green, games master, was grinning. "I'm all right, Jack," he said, rocking back on his chair. "You can't graduate in physical education, and I've got no gown to leave off. You won't be able to flaunt your academic achievements in my face every morning in the hall any more."

Jenny clapped her hands for silence. "Now listen, everyone, if Mr. Hardwick is prepared to consider members of staff's suggestions and alter things that haven't been changed for years, I propose that we have a meeting and make a list of our complaints and submit them to him. Now, who's with me?"

Wayne and I were amongst the handful who put up their hands. The older teachers snorted with disgust and went out.

Jenny arranged a time for the first meeting of the "committee for change", as she called it. "Monday afternoon, after school. You've got the weekend to think up your complaints and suggestions. Mind they're good. It's about time the younger ones among us had their say. Mr. Hardwick's not so old that he'll turn us down flat as old man Browning would have done."

I remembered that I had a dental appointment on Monday.

"Never mind," Jenny said, "we'll pretend you're there and take your support for granted."

Later that afternoon, I carried the globe – the only one the geography department possessed – from the store room to my desk and began to use it. It was dented and no longer spherical.

34

In fact, it resembled a battered ball rather than a model of the earth. It was while I was trying to rotate it to illustrate a point I had made that an idea came to me. Why not ask Brett to lend us his own globe? It was a splendid illuminated affair, and he had often brought it to school in the past for his own use. Sometimes when he'd been in a good mood, he had allowed Wayne and me to use it. Would he, I wondered, let us borrow it again?

It was days since I'd spoken to Brett. I saw him, of course, at morning assembly, standing on the platform, remote and out of reach. I would sit at the back of the hall watching his face, and try to stop myself from thinking of that night on the moors when I'd slept in his arms. I often passed him in the corridor. He usually looked preoccupied, but he would always smile at me briefly but politely, and I began to wonder if that night had ever really happened.

Now I had a reason for seeing him. After school, I asked his secretary if the headmaster was free. He was, she said, and would I like to go in?

I felt ridiculously nervous. He could only refuse my request, I told myself, he couldn't throw me out for insubordination, could he?

He looked startled as I went in. "Hallo, Tracy," he said, then, astonishingly, coloured slightly. "Er – sit down, Miss Johns." He raised his eyebrows and waited for me to speak.

His odd attitude didn't make it any easier for me. "Mr. Hardwick, I hope you don't mind, but –" I licked my lips. Why did I have to be so nervous?

"But, Miss Johns?"

"But do you think you could lend me your illuminated globe for a few days? The school globe is so old and bashed about, it's almost impossible to use. It gets stuck on its own axis and it makes the boys laugh when I have to bang it with something heavy to get it to rotate."

Mr. Hardwick laughed too. In fact he threw back his head

and laughed with such fervour that I began to wonder what I had said that was so funny. It seemed as though he needed to laugh to release some sort of tension inside him.

He stood up and pushed his hands into his pockets. His grin was almost boyish. "It's as well," he said, "that the earth doesn't really get stuck on its own axis. It would take a darned big hammer to get it going again." He looked at his watch. "It's nearly five o'clock. It's Friday and I'm tired. Come on, Miss Johns, I'm getting out of here fast, before that phone rings again. You can come home with me and get that globe. I'll collect my son and meet you at my car."

The headmaster parked his car in front of the school in a privileged position. Members of staff had to park theirs round the back in a corner of the playground. Colin walked by his father's side out of the school entrance doors and grinned when he saw me.

"Come along, Miss Johns," Brett said, "sit in front with me. Colin, go in the back for once."

Colin's grin wavered and disappeared. It was his place in the front, he said.

"It won't always be your place, son," his father told him.

"I suppose you mean when you get married again."

Brett looked at him sharply and then at me, shrugging his shoulders as though he didn't know what the boy was talking about.

"So he's contemplating marriage," I thought miserably, as we drove out of the school grounds into the main road. "What's her name – Elaine? I'll be meeting her in a few minutes. His future wife."

She met us on the doorstep, and her young son was jumping about in the hall behind her. She was slim, she was taller than I was, and she was a blonde. She was wearing slacks and an open-necked blouse. Her blue-framed spectacles emphasised the fairness of her skin and she smiled as Brett passed her on the doorstep. Her smile really impressed me. It was there for

36

Colin and again for me. Brett introduced us and by this time her smile, was tinged with something else, surprise, perhaps, even amazement, but I couldn't detect any animosity or jealousy. She had no reason to be jealous, of course. She had obviously got her employer exactly where she wanted him. She was living in his house, was part of the family and, it seemed, ran his home with great efficiency.

"She's special," he had told me on the moors. "She's a friend. She'll stay." He knew just how to make her stay – by marrying her.

The hall was softly carpeted and the study which Brett called me into was comfortable and masculine. He was dismantling the globe. "Sit down," Brett said, "while I test whether the light still works."

I looked around at the attractive furnishings and the maps of the world which sprawled across the walls. "Sorry it's not very tidy," he commented, and smiled. "I could do with a secretary at home as well as at work!"

"Sorry I can't oblige," I answered. "I just haven't got the secretary mentality. I'm not very tidy myself."

"Then we'd make a fine pair, wouldn't we?" he said to the light bulb he was testing.

I didn't quite know how to take that statement, so I didn't answer. I got up and walked past the papers and pamphlets stacked in piles all over the table and bent down to look at the bookshelves.

They were crammed with atlases and books on geography and geology and I couldn't resist them. I opened one after the other.

"These books are wonderful," I told him.

I pulled out a particularly costly publication, and I flipped excitedly through the pages, stopping to look at the lavish illustrations and colour photographs. Written in bold feminine handwriting on the fly-leaf were the words, "To my darling

Brett, from his devoted and only love, Olivia."

I snapped the book shut and stuffed it back on to the shelf. He came to stand next to me, and my eyes couldn't get above his knees. I could have kicked myself for picking out that book.

"One day," he said quietly, "I'll throw it out. It's been burning a hole in my bookshelves for years."

I stood unsteadily. "They're – they're lovely books, Brett." I turned pink. "I'm sorry, I mean Mr. Hardwick."

"Oh, make it Brett. You like them, Tracy?"

I nodded wistfully. "I could make some fabulous notes with them. They must have cost a fortune."

"They did. Which of them would you like to borrow?"

"Me? Borrow them? But I couldn't do that."

"I'm offering them to you, woman. Now come on, choose."

My hand groped for the book I had pushed back so quickly. "Would you mind very much if I –?"

He pulled the book out. "I'd be delighted." He opened it, ripped out the fly-leaf, screwed the paper into a tight ball and hurled it into the waste-paper basket. "The book's yours. To keep." He put it into my hands.

"To keep, Brett? But I couldn't. . . ." He made an impatient sound, and I said, "You really mean it?"

He dismissed the question with a wave of the hand. "Now help yourself to any of the others. Keep the one I've given you, and return the rest when you've finished with them. No time limit."

Colin stood in the doorway. "Elaine says is Miss Johns staying for dinner because if so she'll have to set for her?"

"That's a good idea. How about it, Tracy?"

"Oh, no, thank you, I couldn't do that."

He turned on me. "Do you spend your whole life saying," he mimicked me, " 'oh, no, I couldn't do that'? This is the third time at least I've heard you use that stupid self-effacing phrase and this will be the third time I'll have proved you

38

could 'do that'." He nodded to Colin, "She'll stay." Colin went out, and told Elaine the answer.

"Now choose your books," Brett said. I did, and by the time I had picked them out and stacked them on the floor beside me, Brett had tested the globe and put it into working order.

"Guard this with your life, Tracy. It cost me a fortune, as you may know."

"Now I feel scared to touch it," I laughed.

He plugged it in and switched on and the globe was flooded with light. "Illuminated, it's physical," he pointed to the mountain ranges and valleys, "off, it's political – all the different countries well defined in bright colours." He carried it to the door. "I'll put it in my car now, and when I run you back, I'll lock it in a cupboard in the geography room and you can use it whenever you like. Bring the books, will you?"

We loaded them into the car, then Elaine called us for dinner. We had it in the long, narrow dining-room which overlooked the garden. The meal was elegantly served, with candles in silver holders, place mats and flowers in crystal vases. I compared the scene with my own bed-sitter, with its scratched and stained table and the old kitchen chair I sat on, and nearly laughed out loud. I thought about my gas-ring and chipped crockery, and couldn't imagine any circumstances whatsoever which would make me invite Brett there. After this, I'd be ashamed to let him see the conditions I lived in.

Colin talked a lot and Brett responded with surprising good humour. He laughed a great deal, which was unusual, as he was normally such a serious person. Elaine rarely spoke, although she smiled all the time. She seemed to have little to say and gave no impression of having any reserves of conversation or intellect. There was a quietness about her, a lack of vitality which I found vaguely irritating, a passive unquestioning acceptance of all things. When she did speak, it was to reprimand her son for bad manners and talking out of turn.

39

She puzzled me. Surely Brett wanted a wife with more to offer? 'But he must know what he's doing,' I thought. It was so obvious he was going to marry her that in my view it was an accomplished fact.

I said I would help with the washing-up, but Brett's answer surprised me. They were hardly the words of a man deeply in love with his housekeeper. "You're my guest, Tracy. It's Elaine's job. That's what I employ her for. So let her get on with it."

Elaine nodded and smiled and got on with it.

"Would you like to see the rest of the house?" Brett asked as we left the dining-room.

He led the way upstairs and I followed, my feet sinking into the thick pile of the stair carpet. The two boys were writhing about on the floor of the entrance hall. Keith, Elaine's son, was about seven years old, and although he was much smaller than Colin, was pummelling him with his fists. Colin was not hitting the boy back, but was trying to defend himself from the badly-aimed blows.

I turned on the landing and looked down at them. "Shouldn't you stop them, Brett?"

"It wouldn't be any good. They'd only start again. Keith won't leave Colin alone. Sometimes Colin turns on him and lets him have it, but the effect on Keith rarely lasts more than a day or two."

"It's going to be awkward for you in the future if they don't get on well together, isn't it?"

He looked at me sharply. "What do you mean, 'going to be, in the future'?"

I tried to hide my confusion. "I mean, going to be awkward whenever they're left alone together."

It seemed that I had managed to put him off the scent because he said, "Oh, we never leave them alone together. Never will."

I left it at that, although I still couldn't understand his off-hand attitude. He showed me his bedroom. It was tidy and neat, but somehow masculine and cold. "A double bed, Brett?" The words were out before I could stop them.

His eyes twinkled. "Yes. Room for a guest, you see."

I blushed and he laughed. "Come and see Elaine's room."

It was pink and feminine and the soft-furnishings and quilted bedcover gave it a touch of luxury. There were velvet scatter cushions on the armchairs, the coffee table was covered in glossy magazines. The polished dining table reflected the colours of the flowers in the vase at the centre.

"It's luxurious," I gasped. "It's beautiful!"

"Why so surprised? I am, after all, her employer. She is also a friend, which makes me want to give her as much comfort as my pocket will allow."

I stopped at the source the thoughts which began to tantalise me.

He showed me Colin's and Keith's rooms, and I said, "It's a large house, Brett. It must have cost a lot of money."

"It wasn't cheap, Tracy. But in the circumstances I had to have plenty of room. Having a housekeeper isn't the same as having a wife."

"No, a housekeeper is better treated than a wife, judging by what I've seen." The words, as they came out, assumed a much deeper meaning than I intended, and I wasn't surprised when Brett turned on me fiercely. "Brett, I didn't mean – I intended it as a joke. I'm sorry."

He relaxed. "I'm sorry too. I misunderstood. For one nasty moment I thought you'd been listening to gossip. Come downstairs, Tracy. I'll show you the playroom."

He opened the door and I stared at the elaborate model railway which occupied most of the room. It rested on two large tables pushed together and the intricate layout of the tracks was made even more complicated by the flyovers and bridges which spanned it.

Brett moved a switch and a tiny locomotive began to circulate. I felt drawn towards it as if it were a magnet. "May I try?"

"Of course." He took my hand and guided it to one of the control units. He told me what to do. Colin came in and watched me.

"That's good, Miss Johns. Now look at me, I'm going to do some shunting. There are the sidings, up that end." I followed his movements and asked if I could try. I managed it first time.

"You're obviously born to it, Tracy," Brett said, putting his arm about my waist. "An enthusiast in the making."

"Fancy a girl liking trains, Dad. I thought only boys did."

"So did I, son. We were wrong."

"Can she come again, Dad?"

"Why not, son?" He smiled at me provocatively. "I can always invite her here to see my model railway – a novel variation on the old 'come and see my etchings' routine."

"Wait till I tell the boys at school. We like Miss Johns' classes. They're fun. Sometimes we laugh so much the teacher in the next room comes in to see what's going on."

Brett's dark eyes swung towards me. "Do you have disciplinary troubles, Miss Johns?"

"Not really, it's just that. . . ."

"I'll say she does, Dad, especially when she makes mistakes."

Brett, now all headmaster, looked at me with concentrated interest. I wanted desperately to put a gag in Colin's mouth.

"Mistakes?"

"Yes, Dad. When we tell her about them, she says she makes them deliberately to see if we're awake. But we don't believe her because she's surprised sometimes when we point them out."

"Colin, please," I whispered, but he went on and on. He was even warming to his subject.

"Do you know, Dad, she loses the board rubber so often

42

she brings her morning paper in with her and tears bits off and screws them up and uses them to rub off the writing on the blackboard."

"Colin, you've got to stop." I'd meant to shout, but it came out as a croak. I looked at Brett, but couldn't understand the expression on his face. He did nothing to rescue me or to stop his son, as he should have done.

"One day, Dad," he laughed at the thought, "she came back from her holiday in the Pennines and the Lake District and showed us some colour slides she had made of the mountains. She pretended they were taken abroad because she didn't tell us where she'd been, and asked us to say what country they were taken in."

I shut my eyes to Brett's raised eyebrows.

"And how many of you guessed, Colin?"

"None of us, Dad. You should have heard some of the answers – Italy, Germany, Norway, even Russia. The best joke of all was, she did it on April Fools' Day and tricked us all."

The shout of laughter Brett gave at this sent trickles of relief down my spine. I'd expected a reprimand, not indulgent mirth.

"Anyway," Colin finished, "we all like Miss Johns' classes."

"I'm glad to hear it. Having ground her teaching reputation into the dust, you now raise her up and put her on a pedestal. The next time I'm feeling low and in need of cheering up, I'll sit in on one of the classes. I might learn something."

I looked at my watch and moved towards the door. "There's no need to run away, Tracy, in spite of my son's lynching session with your character. I apologise for his outspokenness, but I assure you it hasn't adversely affected my opinion of you."

"Thanks, Brett. But I really must go. I never like to outstay my welcome."

"You could never do that where I'm concerned, Tracy." I knew he was only playing the perfect host, so I didn't take him seriously. "But if you must be off, I'll run you back to school to get your car."

When I said good-bye to Elaine, her hand was cool and lifeless, but her smile was warm enough.

In Brett's car, I said, "I like your Elaine."

"You do? I'm glad. She's a very quiet, undemanding person. The best housekeeper I've had, and I've had quite a few. Colin was very difficult when he was younger. It's a very unbalanced life for a child, I suppose, with virtually only one parent."

"But, Brett, one good and loving parent is better by far than two who hate each other's guts, yet stay together, like mine did. Believe me, I know."

His hand left the steering wheel and covered mine as it lay clenched on my knee. "Relax, Tracy."

I opened my hand and he took his away.

I had to say it, because I had to know his reaction. "I think Elaine's very attractive."

"You do? Yes, I've been trying to get her to change to contact lenses. Without her glasses, her looks improve quite a bit. I think I've almost persuaded her."

So I had my answer. Then I remembered I had to thank him for changing the rule about gowns.

He smiled and said, "What was the reaction in the staff room?"

"Very mixed. The older teachers were indignant, the younger ones delighted. We're going to form an action committee." Then I stopped, aghast at what I had told him.

"A *what?*"

"Oh, dear, I shouldn't have told you that, should I?"

"Not if you wanted me to keep my temper. Action committee indeed. Action on what?"

"Making changes," I said in a small voice.

He almost growled with anger.

"But, Brett, you said. . . ."

44

"I *said*. It seems to me that in future I'll have to guard my tongue like a prison warder when you're within hearing distance."

I couldn't stop the tears, although I knew I'd asked for it. I blinked them back as he turned into the school gates and drew up in front of the building. I got out and thanked him for having me.

"I hope you'll come again, Tracy," he said, but I didn't answer, just turned and walked towards the staff car park. He followed carrying my books. "Don't forget these. I haven't seen your car. Had it long?"

"A couple of months. I got it third-hand through my friend Dinah Rowe, who has the bed-sitter across the landing. She knew someone who wanted to sell it." I smiled. "Every day another bit falls off it."

We turned the corner and there it was, standing alone on the concrete. Brett inspected it, looked at the tyres. "Sure it's roadworthy, Tracy? It doesn't look it to me. Did you get someone to vet it for you before you parted with your money?"

"I couldn't afford to pay anyone to do that, and pay for the car."

"If it's not a rude question, how much did it cost?"

I told him. He laughed. "You can't expect much if that's all you paid." He poked about in the bonnet.

"You look as though you know something about a car's inside."

"A fair amount. It used to be a hobby of mine." He lowered the lid. "Don't wait too long before you get it serviced. It needs attention."

"Serviced? It would be far too expensive. I just wait until it goes wrong and hope I'm somewhere near home or near a garage."

He looked horrified. "But that's asking for trouble."

I shrugged, unlocked the door and put the books he had lent me on the front seat. "I'll have to take a chance. Good-bye, Brett, and thank you again."

He watched as I drove along the drive to the main gates, and he waited there until I disappeared from sight.

I kept my dental appointment after school on Monday. Jenny Willis caught me in the corridor as I was leaving the building.

"It's a pity you can't come to the meeting now, Tracy."

"Tell me what you decide, won't you? I'll be with you in spirit, if not in person."

"All right. And we'll take it for granted that you agree with our decisions. Try and get in early in the morning, and I'll have a word with you before assembly."

When I arrived next day, I found Jenny in the staff room. She waved a handwritten list in front of my nose. "This is it, our list of suggestions and complaints to our brand-new head." She put the paper in my hand. "And you're going to be our messenger."

"Messenger? What do you mean?"

"Our go-between, our arbitrator, mediator – oh, you know, the one who does the persuading."

"But why me? I wasn't at the meeting."

"You told me you agreed in advance to all our decisions. You can't go back on that now. We decided to appoint you to the job, and Wayne offered to go with you as moral support."

"But, Jenny, I'm no good at this sort of thing. I get all tongue-tied and nobody listens. It would be much better if you went instead."

"Tracy, you're the one we chose. We – we had our reasons, dear." I raised my eyebrows, and Jenny added, a little uncomfortably, "Well, you managed to talk him into dropping the rule about wearing gowns, so you must have some influence. . . "

"Influence?" Wayne sauntered in. "Who's under the influence? At this time of day?"

"Hallo, Wayne." I held the piece of paper out to him. "I don't want to see the head about this, Wayne. Can't you go instead?"

"I'm coming with you, pet, aren't I? You don't have to worry when Uncle Wayne's there to hold your hand."

I began to read. "We, the undersigned members of staff, should be glad if improvements could be made to the following:

"Science laboratories: New equipment urgently needed. Car parking facilities for staff: an enlargement of parking space is an urgent necessity. Language laboratory required for English department. Gym changing rooms require alteration. More staff meetings requested."

There followed six signatures. Jenny handed me a pen. "Add your name, Tracy."

I hesitated. "You're asking for too much at once, you know. He won't like this."

"Go on, Tracy, sign it."

I knew I had to. There was no alternative. I wrote my name with a shaky hand.

"You will take it in to him for us, won't you? Don't let us down, Tracy."

Mrs. Wilkinson, Brett's secretary, gave me an appointment to coincide with my first free period next morning. I spent a restless night, trying to think of answers to the questions I knew the headmaster would ask. When I did sleep, I dreamed that he was chasing me out of the school building, waving a piece of paper and telling me never to set foot inside the place again.

I arrived at school heavy-eyed and nervous. Wayne took my hand as we walked along the corridor after assembly and stood outside the head's door. I lifted my hand to knock, but Wayne caught it.

"Wait, Tracy. Look, sweetie, I think it best if you go in on your own. Won't do much good if I come in with you.

I'll only rub him up the wrong way. You know me. Anyway, I'm being a good boy at the moment, aren't I? I want that promotion. So you go in, Tracy. I'll be with you in spirit."

"But, Wayne, you can't walk out on me now. I'm dreading this, but I'm not turning coward. You *must* come, Wayne. Please!"

He squeezed my hand and walked away. "Let me know how you get on, won't you?" he called over his shoulder.

I was almost in tears. I tapped at the heavy wooden door and waited for the voice to invite me in.

CHAPTER III

My legs felt strangely weak as I walked into the study. The headmaster looked at me, his eyes narrow and hard, and I wondered if he could see how nervous I was. He motioned me to a chair and went on with his writing, while I sat turning and twisting the piece of paper with my fingers. He threw down his pen, sat back and asked, "Well, Miss Johns?"

The moment had come and I was speechless. He waited for me to say something and smiled, probably to give me encouragement.

"Having trouble getting started?"

"It's – I – well, it's about this." In desperation, I put the piece of paper on his desk.

He picked it up and turned it over. "It's a bit mutilated, isn't it? What has it done to deserve that treatment?" He read it and as the words sank in, his frown deepened. His thick black eyebrows were almost touching over the bridge of his nose when he looked at me. "Now I understand the reason for your state of nerves. You might well be shaking in your shoes."

"I did tell you, Mr. Hardwick, about the committee we had formed. Well, they had their first meeting yesterday and that's what they decided."

"Why 'they', not 'we'?"

"I'm sorry, I should have said 'we'. I agreed with everything they decided. I told them I would."

He seemed puzzled. He put the paper down. "Since you seem to be acting as official carrier pigeon between the rest of the staff and myself, kindly tell me exactly what took place at that meeting."

"I don't know, Mr. Hardwick, I wasn't there. I went to the dentist."

His voice rose impatiently. "Then why for goodness' sake are you here? Why didn't one of the others come instead?"

"Because they nominated me as their representative."

"In your absence?" I nodded. "Without your consent?"

"Well, I had agreed in advance with all their decisions."

"A very dangerous thing to do."

"So you see, I had to keep my word. I had to come since they chose me."

He narrowed his eyes thoughtfully. "I'd love to know why. It's obvious you're almost inarticulate in circumstances like this, and quite useless as a spokesman."

I broke in eagerly, "That's what I told them, but it made no difference."

"No doubt they decided from the confidences you've let slip that you 'have my ear', as the saying goes, and that I'll listen to and agree with anything you say." He drummed on the desk with his fingers. "How do they know I won't go deaf where you're concerned and throw you out of my room?"

I smiled weakly. "You wouldn't do that, Mr. Hardwick. You're too gentlemanly."

He rose and walked slowly round his desk to stand in front of me, hands in his pockets. "Don't be too sure of that, Miss Johns. Don't challenge me. I warn you, my gentlemanliness is only skin-deep."

I flushed and looked away. He stood there gazing down at me for a few moments, then returned to his chair.

"Anyway, they nominated Wayne to come with me." I stopped in horror, realising I'd slipped up again.

He was on to it straight away. "You see, you can't stop yourself letting things out, can you?"

"I told you once before not to trust me," I answered bitterly.

"And why didn't Wayne," he gave the word an unpleasant

sound, "come with you? Surely I heard his voice outside? What did he do, give you Dutch courage, then leave you in the lurch? Why didn't he come in and do his own dirty work?"

I knew the answer, but couldn't tell him. There was a long silence while he studied the list, then he dropped it on his desk as though it was covered in germs.

"I must tell you that I've already had some adverse reaction to the one change I've dared to make to school tradition. Dr. Winsor came to see me about the abandoning of academic gowns. He objected to my ruling. He also said he didn't like the way things were going in this school nowadays. He told me there was a group of teachers who were troublemakers, and he named you as one of them, Tracy."

"He called me a troublemaker? But all I'm suggesting, with the support of the others, is that a few changes would make the school more up-to-date. And asking for an improvement in working conditions for the staff. After all," my eyes looked for his, "I remember your telling me – once – that you would like to make some changes yourself if you ever got the chance, so would he call you a troublemaker?"

Brett rose and walked about the room. "What we're up against in a school like this, you know, is tradition, clinging to the past, 'what was good enough for Grandpa is good enough for me' attitude." He stood in front of me. "I have to tread carefully, Tracy, slowly, tactfully, subtly. Now I'm in command and have the power to alter people's ways, their lives even, I must use that power wisely and diplomatically." He pulled me to my feet, and kept my hands in his. "Will you trust me, Tracy? Will you hold in check your very natural and youthful desire to improve things and restrain your colleagues instead of being used by them for their own ends?" I tried to take my hands from his, but he held them fast. "Will you have patience? Wait a while, only a little while. We'll feel our way together, shall we? I'm new to this, too, you know. I'll need your help."

He dropped my hands, walked back to his seat and picked up the piece of paper. "I'll look into these, but I'm not making any promises. That's all, Miss Johns, thank you for coming to see me."

Jenny met me in the staff room at lunch time. "Tracy, what happened? Did the head agree to everything?"

"Everything, Jenny? You must be joking. He wouldn't commit himself on anything, not one thing. All he said was he'd look into them."

"Well, I like that! We'll have to put more pressure on him."

I put my hand on her arm. "No, don't do that. He told me he's new to the job, and wants to feel his way. He said we must be patient. Let's give him time to think about things."

Jenny shrugged. "All right, but we're not giving him much time. These things have needed attention long enough. We can't be patient indefinitely."

"Next time," I said, "you'd better go and see him yourself. I wasn't much good, I'm afraid."

"But, Tracy, we sent you because we heard – we thought you two –" She spotted another teacher and called, "I want to see you, Pat. Half a minute. Well, all right, Tracy, thanks for trying anyway."

Wayne kept out of my way all day and I wondered if he was feeling ashamed of himself. But when he turned up at my door that evening, he was as brash as ever.

"Why are you here?" I gave him a freezing look.

"To see my best girl, pet. Whyever else?"

"Well, you're not very welcome."

"I suppose you've still not forgiven me for leaving you to sink or swim at the head's door this morning?"

"No. And as a result nothing came of the interview."

"So Jenny told me. You know," he sat in my armchair, "I thought you had more influence with him than that. Rumour has it you're as thick as thieves."

"If anyone's thick, you are, Wayne. Can you really imagine it? I've been warned off him enough times, and anyway, there's his housekeeper. It's a hundred per cent certain he's going to marry her. She's attractive and not far off his age."

"And how do you know that, sweetie? Have you met her?"

I could have kicked myself, and blushed furiously, a fact which Wayne obviously noted with interest. "Yes, well, I met her the other day. I went to his house —"

"Did you now? Tell me more."

"It was only to borrow his globe. The school one's useless and I asked him if we could use his."

"So that's why it's back in the geography room. You mean he actually allowed you to borrow it? Consider yourself highly honoured. He used to treat it like solid gold when he brought it to school in the past. So it seems you've some influence, after all."

"I tell you I haven't, Wayne." I nearly added 'unfortunately', but stopped just in time.

My expression must have given my thoughts away, because Wayne said, "It's no good looking like that, Tracy." He waggled his engagement finger at me. "And it's no good looking for a ring from him. Where marriage is concerned, he's let it be known that not only is his number permanently out of order, he's ex-directory, just not in the book."

"There's no need to tell me that," I snapped.

He rubbed his chin and contemplated me as I sat at the table trying to make notes. "All the same, it's interesting. . . ."

"What is?"

He stretched lazily and stood up. "Oh, the things one hears. Well, since you seem determined to give me the cold shoulder, I'll be off."

"Sorry, Wayne," I smiled and went up to him, touched his lapels, "I'm not in a very good mood."

"You're telling me." He kissed me. "All is forgiven, then?"

I nodded. He stood at the door and nodded towards Dinah's

room. "And where's honey-girl tonight? Out with her boy-friend?"

"Oh, one of them, probably. She's got a selection. Why, do you want your name put on her list?"

"At first sight, yes. But I'd have to – er – get to know her a little more – intimately, shall we say, before I made up my mind."

I pushed him out. "Oh, men," I said, and waved as he went down the stairs.

I was closing my class for morning break a few days later, when the headmaster's secretary knocked and entered. "Miss Johns, a message from Mr. Hardwick. He wishes to see you at once in his study. Sorry about the short notice."

I looked at my watch. "But it's break-time, Mrs. Wilkinson. Perhaps he doesn't realise that. Would he mind if I had my coffee first?"

"Sorry, Miss Johns, but he did say at once. He sent me off for my coffee, so I don't think he's forgotten." She lowered her voice so that the boys wouldn't hear. "I shouldn't keep him waiting, he seemed in a bit of a mood."

I dismissed the class and went quickly to Brett's room. He looked up immediately, and his face was black with anger. He didn't even tell me to sit down before he attacked me.

"It's as well you've been quick. As it is, I feel I could almost tear you apart." He curled his fingers stiffly and shook them at me.

I recoiled. "What have I done now?"

"Done? I'll tell you what you've done. I've just returned from a prolonged session with the Chief Education Officer. He informed me, in the most hypocritical language possible, that there is circulating round the town a rumour that I," he jabbed a finger at his chest, "am having an illicit relationship with a woman member of my staff, that we spent the night together on the moors, that we are now having a secret affair,

54

and if I don't marry her soon and make an 'honest woman' of her, my position as headmaster of this school may be in serious jeopardy. That, coming after the fact that I have only just succeeded in living down the bad name given to me by my late wife, is surely enough to make any man want to rip the person responsible apart!"

He stopped for breath and I started to mouth some words in my own defence, but he crunched over my feeble and hasty denials like a garden roller over a beetle. "The woman we are discussing, in case it has not yet penetrated your thick skull, is not my housekeeper, which is what I would have expected, people's minds being what they are, but you, *you*." He came round the desk. "Now do you see where the indiscretions of your juvenile tongue have got you – and me?" He walked away. "There have been pure-minded lady councillors calling at the Education Offices to tell the C.E.O. I should be sacked. There have been irate parents telephoning to complain about the disastrous effect I must be having on their precious sons' morals. There have been others, mostly pious old gentlemen, who have demanded *your* dismissal."

I had to sit down. Now everything was falling into place – Wayne's cryptic remarks, Jenny's idea of sending me to the head to use my 'influence'. "But why blame me?" It was all I could get out.

"Who else? Who else could it be? I've already discovered to my horror just how unguarded you can be. Is nothing sacred to you? Did you have to blab like an ingenuous babe to all and sundry about that very, very innocent night we spent on the moors?"

I knew what was coming. I bowed my head and waited for the axe to swing and decapitate my dream. When the blow came, it was swift and deadly. And final.

"What," he taunted, "did your tiny adolescent mind read into those meaningless moments in the mist? What romantic nonsense did you dream up in your girlish thoughts with the

55

aid of your over-active imagination?" His smile was twisted. "Are you so naïve as to think that a few words of comfort from a man in the darkness meant he was carried away with love for you?"

I could find no answer. I shook my head. "I can only say that I told no one, Mr. Hardwick."

He waited, tensed, apparently wanting to believe me. "No one? Not a single soul? Can you swear to that?"

I remembered Dinah, Wayne. "No," I whispered, "I can't swear to it."

He banged his fist on the desk. "I knew I was right! I knew it. You are the source of all the lies and slander."

I stood up. I had to get out of that room before it suffocated me. I didn't wait to be dismissed. I went to the door, but turned. I had to say something in my own defence. "I am not naïve. I am not an adolescent. I'm a mature, fully-grown adult, and as such have my imagination under strict control. I never allow myself to imagine love where none exists. I had good practice in quelling that sort of nonsense as a child, when I listened to my *loving* parents quarrelling."

I wished he would look at me, but he was doodling with a pencil on his blotter. I wondered if he was even listening.

"Please don't feel under any obligation to me because of those moments in the mist. They were as meaningless to me as they were to you." He pressed so hard on his pencil that the point broke and he flung it down on the desk. "I'm sure I'm not the source of those rumours. How could I be when the whole incident was so trivial, so – so insignificant?"

I ran out of the room along the corridor to the cloakroom, where I dried my eyes and powdered my nose. I taught my classes like a teaching-machine for the rest of the day. I used the illuminated globe for the last time that afternoon. Its owner could take it home again for all I cared.

If only I could be sure in my own mind that I was not to blame for those rumours! I would ask Wayne and Dinah how

56

many people they had told.

I dismissed the last class of the afternoon and talked to the boys who lingered round my desk so irritably they took offence, and stalked off. I was sorry because they weren't used to that sort of treatment from me, but I had to be alone to think. I hoped to catch Wayne before he went home.

I lifted the headmaster's globe from the desk and carried it into the small store-room attached to the geography room. I lowered it carefully to the shelf and turned away to the door. My elbow caught the wooden stand which supported the globe, and it toppled. I swung round too late to intercept it in its headlong fall. It hit the wooden floor with a horrifying crash, and I could only stand and stare as it lay like a wounded animal, on its side.

I crouched down, my heart pounding, and inspected the globe without daring to touch it. At first sight it didn't seem damaged. I lifted it and heard an ominous chink of glass inside. The wooden stand had a split across it like a fissure caused by an earthquake. The polythene sphere was dented into a saucer shape where it had hit the floor.

My hand was shaking as I pushed the plug at the end of the flex into a nearby wall socket. It didn't light, of course, and that confirmed that the bulb inside was smashed. I wanted to run away and hide. "Guard it with your life," Brett had said. "It's worth pounds."

"Consider yourself honoured to be allowed to borrow it," Wayne had told me. And now I'd broken it and let Brett Hardwick down again. I had to tell him, and the sooner the better. I had to get it off my conscience. I went to the door and looked up and down the corridor. I must have concentrated on him powerfully hard because there he was, coming towards me.

"Still here, Miss Johns?" His curtness didn't help. "It's late."

Now I must tell him, now, not tomorrow. "Mr. – Mr. Hardwick, would you mind coming into the geography room?"

"Why?" He stopped in his tracks, probably sensing trouble from my expression. "Something wrong?"

I nodded my head towards the store-room and he moved past me through the doorway. I couldn't get the words out to tell him. I followed slowly, and heard his explosive curse.

He stood there staring, as I had done, then he bent and examined the globe and put it down again.

"Who did this?" I couldn't make myself answer. "One of the boys?"

I had to tell him. I whispered, "I did it, Mr. Hardwick."

"You did it? *You* did it?" He seemed beside himself with rage. "For what purpose? A subtle but effective way of getting your own back?"

"*What?* How can you think that?" I was desperate to convince him. "It was an accident, Mr. Hardwick, an accident, it was an accident. . . ." I had to make him believe me.

I must have convinced him in the end. "Stop it," he ordered. "I suppose I'll have to accept what you say. I've discovered one thing about you — you may be inconsequential, but you're compulsively honest."

"I'm terribly sorry, Mr. Hardwick. I'll pay for the repair, or if necessary, replace it."

"Don't be an idiot, Miss Johns. This thing cost pounds."

He lifted the twisted carcase of the globe, carried it into the classroom and lowered it tenderly on to the teacher's desk. I stood beside him as he removed the sphere from the broken stand. With the infinite care of a mother tending her baby, he eased the two halves of the globe apart.

As they disengaged from each other, some pieces of glass from the smashed light bulb fell out. Spontaneously, I dived forward to catch them. Some larger pieces dropped on to my palm. Instinctively I closed my other hand down to stop them falling to the floor and breaking into even smaller pieces.

I felt the blood spurting out and watched fascinated as it gathered and dripped steadily downwards.

"Oh-oh," I said, in a sad but interested voice. "Now look."

The headmaster turned and saw the blood and drew in his breath.

"My God, she's done it again." He put the globe halves down, took my hands and moved me towards the waste-paper basket. He turned them over, palms down, until the glass dropped into the rubbish below. Then he examined my hands closely.

"As I thought, some tiny pieces still clinging. Come to the sink." He pulled me towards it, blood dripping liberally over the floor, ran the cold water and told me to hold my hands under it until he got back. "Make sure every single piece of glass is washed away."

The ice-cold water flooded over my hands, cleansing them of the blood and chips of glass. As my skin cleared I discovered that only one hand was injured, but the cut itself was spectacular – a clear, semi-circular incision which stretched half-way round my right palm.

"Oh, dear," I muttered, "I wish I were properly left-handed."

Brett had returned and was fishing inside the first aid box. "What do you mean, properly?"

He inspected the wound and snipped off three or four inches of adhesive plaster.

"Well, I write with my left hand and always use my left pockets, but use my right hand for everything else."

"And how did that come about?"

"Well, when I was small and starting to do things for myself, my mother told me she always transferred everything from my left to my right hand. No one told her she was wrong. She said I battled with her for years, but she won. Now I'm never quite sure which hand to use."

"Really? Now that could have set up all kinds of conflicts inside you and – er – account for a lot of things."

I was on the defensive immediately, being very sensitive

about my left-handed inclinations. "What do you mean? What things?"

He was cleaning the cut again and his face was hidden. "Oh, your general behaviour, your unpredictability, your accident-proneness, amongst other things."

He began to probe, trying presumably to see if the cut was entirely free of glass.

"The other things, no doubt, being my untrustworthiness, my habit of blurting out secrets, my –" I bit my lip as he started to hurt me.

Tears welled up and dripped down my cheeks and one landed on the hand he was tending. He looked up to the source of the tear-drop and tutted. "Mature, fully-grown adults don't cry when they're hurt, Miss Johns."

His heartless, mocking tone was the last straw. That tear-drop was joined by many more, but he merely pulled my hand nearer to him and away from the salt tears which were now coming thick and fast. I couldn't tell him why I was crying. I couldn't say that his nearness unnerved me, his mockery maddened me and the touch of his hands unbalanced me. Nor could I tell him that the hurt he had inflicted on me that morning exceeded by far the superficial cut he was trying to repair.

"It's all right," I sobbed, "leave it alone. I'll put some plaster on it myself." I jerked my hand away and he drew in his lips.

"For the record, Miss Johns, I would remind you that I'm in charge here. You will therefore do as I say. You will let *me* put the plaster on, when I'm ready to do so." He moved a chair towards me. "Sit down."

I sat down. He applied a smear of healing cream and pressed the long strip of plaster over it. I was still crying, because I couldn't stop. The hardness of his profile and the unfeeling glint in his eyes made sure of that. He put my bandaged hand from him.

"For heaven's sake, girl, control yourself. It can't hurt that much."

His lack of sympathy made me worse. It also brought out the worst in me. It made me forget my very junior place on the staff.

I lifted my watery eyes to his and stared him out. "You're hard, Mr. Hardwick. Your name suits you. You're as hard inside as flint. I don't wonder," I muttered into my undamaged hand, "that your wife called you c-cruel, and walked out on you. Any woman would."

There was a sharp movement beside me and the fingers that gripped my shoulders were so bruising I cried out in pain. He shook me and said, between his teeth, "If I weren't convinced you were suffering from a mild form of shock, I'd – I'd. . . ."

He gave me one last shake and the pressure ceased as suddenly as it had started. I heard footsteps retreating and I knew I was alone. The emptiness of the classroom echoed my sobs back to me. It was a sound which seemed to my lonely ears so futile and so pointless that I stopped. "What's the use," the little child in me asked, "of crying when there's no one to cry to, no one to answer your call for help?"

The globe lay on the desk, still in pieces. It struck a chord deep down inside me and I longed to be able to put the thing together again, take it to him and say, "There's your world, Mr. Hardwick, rebuilt and whole, and even better than it used to be."

I gathered my belongings, picked up my handbag and went to the cloakroom. I worked on my messy cheeks and bleak eyes and thought it was wonderful what cosmetics could do.

Wayne called after me from the other end of the corridor. "Tracy, wait for me." He caught me up. "What are you doing here so late?"

"What about yourself?" I snapped. I was too depressed to rise to his brashness and hurried on. He caught me up again. "What's the hurry?" Then he saw my face, and I realised that cosmetics couldn't hide pain in the eyes. "Who's upset you, pet? What's wrong?"

I shook my head, wanting to shake him off my trail. "Nothing. I'm going home." I ran ahead and he caught me up in the car park.

"There is, Tracy. Look, I'll come to your place this evening and we'll talk it out. Would that help?"

I paused with my key in the car door. Perhaps it would. At least I could ask him how much he had told other people about that night on the moors. I knocked my damaged hand on the window handle and winced. He saw the plaster.

"How come? Had a fight?"

"Yes, with the world. The whole world. It fell to pieces at my feet."

"You're kidding. You must be. You haven't broken golden boy's globe?" I nodded. "My God!" He stared. "I'm not surprised if he got rough with you. He prizes that beyond almost everything, the exception being his precious son."

Tears threatened. "I know. You can imagine how I felt when I saw it fall. I – I caught it with my elbow." I explained how I got the cut on my hand.

"Will you be able to drive the car?"

I slid my hands round the steering wheel. "I think I'll manage, thanks."

Wayne closed the door for me and raised his hand. "Take care, pet. See you later."

I moved along the drive to the school gates, passing the main entrance on the way. Brett was carrying the damaged globe to his car. I crunched slowly along the gravel towards the gates, and his car caught me up as I waited to join the main road which went past the school. I looked in my driving mirror and caught a glimpse of his hard, handsome face staring at the back of my car. In some peculiar fashion our eyes met in the mirror and I grew flustered. I revved the engine, looked left, forgot to look right and moved out to join the main stream of traffic. A car approaching from the right set up a furious hooting as it swerved outwards and just missed my bonnet.

The headmaster, still behind me, flashed his lights madly and as he overtook me gave me the benefit of the filthiest look in his extensive repertoire. I wouldn't be sure, but I think he added a few swear words for good measure.

I knew I would have a lecture from him in the morning on the driving habits of young women teachers, especially partially left-handed ones, and how they ought not to be allowed on the roads.

When Wayne arrived after tea, Dinah was with me. She was reclining in my armchair and her feet were resting on the table. Her long, shapely legs were revealed from top to painted toenail, but she lowered them when Wayne came in. Not before his eyes had lapped them up, though, like a cat tackling its first saucer of milk for weeks.

"You've been introduced, of course," I waved them together and although their hands didn't make contact, their eyes did. "Sit down, Wayne." I pointed to a dining chair.

Their eyes detached from each other, and Wayne remembered me. "How's the hand, Tracy?"

I said it throbbed a bit, but I was bearing up. Then I told him about my stormy interview with the headmaster that morning and about the rumour which was circulating round the town and which everyone seemed to know about except me.

"I've already asked Dinah, Wayne, now I'll ask you – how much have you told other people about what happened to me that night on the moors?"

"I've told no one, no one at all, sweetie, and I mean that. Let's face it, it wasn't worth the telling, was it? You and the acting head, marooned in the mist with twelve boys. Not even if you stretched your imagination to its limits could you visualise anything, but anything, happening."

I believed him, and I was more puzzled than ever. "Dinah
63

says she hasn't told anyone either. After all, there was so little to tell."

Wayne smiled at Dinah and jerked his thumb towards me. "She actually sounds disappointed, doesn't she?"

They laughed. I didn't. "But, Wayne, the slanders that have been going round!" When I told them all the things Brett and I were supposed to have done, Wayne roared with laughter.

"Innocent little Tracy, having an affair with golden boy!" He slapped the table top. "Good grief, if anybody ever penetrated his defences again, they'd only find more defences underneath. It's a dead loss, pet."

They enjoyed the joke, and I left them to make some coffee in the downstairs kitchen. When I carried the tray into my room, Wayne had moved closer to Dinah.

"You both look so cosy it's a pity to disturb you. Do you really want this coffee?"

"Of course, pet." Wayne took two cups and handed one to Dinah. "It'll taste like nectar, won't it, Dinah? After all, look who's made it, golden boy's woman."

"Poor old Tracy." Dinah drank her coffee. "She needs protecting, doesn't she? Such a little innocent at heart, too."

I asked Wayne, thoughtfully, "What does inconsequential mean, Wayne?"

"Let me see, it means someone who does something without thinking about the consequences of that action, without considering the possible result. A bit like a kid. Why?"

"Oh. That's what Mr. Hardwick called me. He also said I was unpredictable and accident-prone. And an idiot."

Wayne laughed again. "He really does think a lot of his most junior geography teacher! Any time Miss Johns wants a reference to get another job, just ask the headmaster. He'll be so glad to get rid of you, he'll make it good enough to frame. That's the way to push out someone you'd rather be without — give 'em a good reference and persuade the other fellow to

64

take 'em." He looked at his watch. "Think I'll get me a drink and drown my sorrows."

"Have one for me, Wayne, and drown my sorrows, too."

He squeezed my hand and ran down the stairs. "Never mind, pet," he called, "bear up. Golden boy can't throw you out of your job – not without the consent of the education committee!"

Next morning my car refused to start. It had been raining all night and as there were no garages provided for tenants' cars, mine had to stand in the driveway. The damp must have got into the engine and made it sluggish. Another tenant – a pleasant young man I'd often met on the stairs – managed to get it going for me. The delay made me late and I drove above the speed limit all the way along the main road, checking in my mirror all the time that I was not being followed by a police car. I joined the only length of de-restricted road on my journey and put my foot down, stretching the engine of my car to its limits. I hoped to make up lost minutes and arrive in time to take my class. I knew I had missed assembly. I visualised a roomful of rowdy boys and remembered how annoyed the headmaster had been when Wayne was missing on the first day of term.

Traffic was light and I approached the crossroads, cursing the roundabout which sprawled across my path. The road surface was slippery with the overnight rain and I should have slowed down. I didn't. My bandaged hand slipped out of position on the steering wheel, the car swerved to the left out of control. I panicked, tried to correct its sideways lurch, but only made matters worse. Seconds before I hit the tree, I remembered to brake. The car jarred to a standstill and rattled and shook to a frightening silence.

CHAPTER IV

MY heart was pounding, I was gasping for breath, but I was in one piece. I forced the door open, pushing it against the long grass, and got out to inspect the damage. The bumper was twisted out of shape and firmly locked round the tree trunk. The radiator was badly dented, but apart from that, the car seemed to have escaped.

I looked up and down an empty road. I would even have welcomed the sight of that police car I had dreaded meeting earlier. I walked along the road, making for a splash of red in the near distance. As I hoped, it was a telephone kiosk. I found some coins and dialled and got through to Mrs. Wilkinson. I explained what had happened, and was telling her the number of my classroom when I heard a voice ask, "Who's that?"

She answered him. "Miss Johns has had an accident with her car," and the phone must have been snatched from her hand because the next thing I heard was, "Tracy? Brett here. What's happened?"

I told him and his tuts irritated my ear. "I could see this coming," he ground out. "Where are you?"

I said, "Don't worry, Mr. Hardwick. I'll wait for a car to come along and give me a lift. Then I suppose I'll have to contact a garage to tow my car into town. I can't phone because I've run out of change."

"Tracy, I insist, tell me exactly where you are."

I told him.

"Give me –" he must have looked at his watch, "fifteen minutes."

He slammed down the receiver. There was a police car parked near by when I got back to my car. Two policemen were lifting and pushing it free of the tree it was nuzzling against so lovingly.

"Your car, miss? Are you all right?"

"I'm fine, thanks. It's my car I'm worried about. I've just been using the phone."

"Called a garage, miss?"

"No. A – a friend's coming, actually. I didn't have enough change to call a garage."

They released the handbrake and manoeuvred the car off the verge and on to the road. "Try the starter, miss. See if she works."

The car fired into life. I gave them my brightest smile. "It works, it works!"

"You should have it looked at, miss. Might be some internal damage, especially in a car as old as this."

They looked up and down the road. "Don't stay here too long, will you? You could be causing an obstruction."

Brett's car slowed down when he spotted the police car. As he came to a stop, I thanked the policemen for their help and they left us.

Brett threw himself out of his car and glanced at his watch. "Ten minutes," he said. "It's a wonder my fingers aren't permanently crossed after this. In the end I had to meet one," he meant a police car, "but it didn't matter by then." He looked me over. "First, how are you? Any damage?" I shook my head. "You seem a bit shaken, but I expected that." He lifted my injured hand.

"It slipped on the steering wheel," I told him. "The roads are wet and I veered left and went on to the verge."

He dropped my hand and shook his head. "It's all so familiar, so familiar." He looked around. "The only thing that's different is the location. No moors, no mist. And no boys." He tutted. "You're hopeless, aren't you?" Only his smile

67

softened his words.

"It was an accident, Mr. Hardwick," I wailed, "an accident."

"I've heard that before, too." He opened the bonnet of my car and peered inside. Ten minutes later, he was still there and I began to shiver. It was not a cold morning, but I couldn't stop shivering. "W-will you be long, Mr. Hardwick? M-my class will be waiting."

"I've taken care of your class." He closed the bonnet, and looked through the driver's window. "How's the steering?"

"A bit loose."

"M'm. Needs attention, like the rest of it. What's the matter, are you cold?"

I nodded. "I c-can't st-stop shaking."

He smiled a secret smile and murmured, "That's familiar, too." His eyes held mine. "Where's the sleeping bag, Tracy?"

"At home, Brett." I tried to pull my eyes away from his, but he clung to them. "But I wish I had it here," I whispered.

He straightened at last. His voice returned to normal as he said, "We've got to move from here. Do you feel fit to drive?"

"I'll have to, won't I?" I pressed the starter, and it fired into life.

He moved away. "You go on in front, Tracy. I'll follow close behind. I won't overtake you, I won't leave you. Will that help?"

I nodded and pulled away from the roadside, and he drove behind me all the way to the school. I took my car round the back while he drew up near the front entrance.

He was standing at the door of his study as I walked along the corridor. "Come in, Miss Johns."

I went in, afraid of what was coming. He told me to sit down, so I did. My legs were weak and my head felt odd.

"My secretary's getting us some coffee." I smiled my thanks, and he began to pace about the room. I wondered why he was so restless.

68

"Thank you, Brett, I mean Mr. Hardwick, for coming to my rescue."

His next words were in the nature of a broadside, and sent me swerving to the left again. "Frankly, Miss Johns, I think you're a menace on the roads."

It took me a few moments to recover from his attack. "Are — are you referring to last night, Mr. Hardwick, when —"

"When you didn't observe one of the basic rules of the road, that is, looking *both* ways before emerging from a turning, yes. Also that day on the moors. And this morning." He faced me and his eyes were strangely anxious. "I'm appalled — and terrified — at your low standard of driving. Who taught you?"

"Dinah, my friend in the next bed-sitter. She had an old car at the time. She's sold it since."

"As I thought, a friend. Not a properly qualified driving instructor."

I was horrified. "I couldn't have afforded the fees. Anyway, I can't be that bad. I passed second time."

"Sure it wasn't the twenty-second?"

I drew in my lips and started to get up and go, but Mrs. Wilkinson came in with the coffee. She asked me how I felt, told me I looked pale and hoped the coffee would help me feel better. I wanted to say, "Your boss's insults certainly don't", but I sipped my coffee instead.

When we were alone again, Brett drummed on the desk with his fingers — long, tapered fingers, I noticed, and supple hands, and I longed to feel their touch on me. . . .

"Tracy." He whispered my name. Those fingers stopped drumming and I tore my fascinated eyes away. "Come out of your dream."

One of those hands stretched towards me. "Come over here." The hand stiffened in mid-air. "No, no, stay where you are."

He walked the length of the room and back. "Tracy, I want to talk to you. I have some explaining to do relevant to our —

discussion yesterday morning. Provided you've no other engagement, I want you to come here to my study at four-fifteen this afternoon. Can you do that?"

"Yes, Brett."

"Good. Now that car of yours, it needs attention. Would you let me look at it some time? As I told you, messing about with cars used to be a hobby of mine."

"But, Mr. Hardwick, I couldn't bother you with –"

"It wouldn't be a bother." He smiled grimly. "I almost regard it as my duty to other road users to get that car into safe working order. Now, let me see, we'll have to fix a time." He flipped through the pages of his diary, paused as though a thought had struck him, looked at me and snapped the diary shut. He became vague. "Yes, well, it depends on Elaine. I'll consult her first."

So now I knew. Elaine called the tune where engagements were concerned.

"You'll have to take the car to a garage to get the bumper straightened and the radiator put right. It needs a certain amount of brute force. I can't supply that, but I do love fiddling about inside engines." He smiled and looked at his watch. "Now, are you feeling better, Miss Johns?"

I took the hint and stood up. "Yes, thank you, Mr. Hardwick. Thank you again for coming to my rescue. And for the coffee."

He waved away my gratitude. "All in the interests of the school. Can't afford to lose a teacher, especially one the boys seem to like so much."

He smiled and I smiled back. "This afternoon?" he said.

I nodded and walked to the staff room feeling like a Hovercraft, with a cushion of air beneath my feet. Most of the staff were there enjoying the last few minutes of the morning break.

Wayne came towards me. "Well, well, Madame has arrived. Did your alarm let you down?" He gave a sweeping bow. "Coffee, Madame?"

I laughed. I would have laughed at anything at that moment. After all, I had just made a date with the headmaster. "I've had it, thanks. With Mr. Hardwick." What did I care if they put the wrong construction on that bit of information?

"Oh yes? Did he tell you off for being late, then sugar the pill by giving you coffee?"

Jenny came over to me. "Where've you been, Tracy? I was landed with your class. You should have seen Mr. Hardwick's face when he found them playing merry hell unattended. You could hear him shouting for Miss Johns at the other end of the school. He caught me in here and shoved me in front of him like a hostage and told me to sit there until you came. He gave them some work, threatened them with murder if they weren't quiet and left me to it."

"Sorry, Jenny, but I had an accident. My car got involved with a tree. I found a phone box and told the head's secretary and he overheard the conversation. He came in his car to get me out of the mess, but two policemen got there first."

"So that's where he was going when he rushed out of the building like a scalded cat." Pete Green, the P.E. teacher, was looking at me with an assessing stare. "Playing Sir Galahad to our little Miss Johns. I've heard a few rumours. . . ."

"Shut up, Pete." Wayne turned on him and Pete pretended to hide behind his hands. "Believe it or not, golden boy is taking a fatherly interest in our Tracy." There were hoots of laughter from the male members of staff. "It's true. He told me himself." More laughter. I turned away, disgusted. My silver thread of happiness was beginning to tarnish.

"The trouble with old cars," Dr. Winsor murmured, half to himself, "is that they're not to be trusted on the roads."

"The trouble with women drivers, especially young, attractive ones," Mike Smith grinned, "is that they're not to be trusted on the roads."

I made a dive at him with my folders and he ducked towards the door. "When you passed your driving test, Tracy,

I bet you wore your most seductive outfit – swimming suit, perhaps, brief and to the point?" I lunged at him again, but he managed to put the door between us.

Wayne caught me round the waist and pushed me into a chair. "It's not fair to tease a small defenceless infant, is it? Calm down, sweetie. You can't go to your class breathing fire and fury like that."

I struggled out of the chair and made for the door. "Why does everyone treat me as though I'm infantile, irresponsible and half-witted?"

Wayne opened the door for me. "I wouldn't say that, Tracy. Let's say we're indulgent where you're concerned. We wouldn't insult a little thing like you. You know what you are, don't you? – the teachers' pet, especially the male ones."

I snorted, which for some reason made him laugh again, and went to my class.

Unbelievably, the day passed. At four-fifteen, I asked Mrs. Wilkinson if the headmaster was free. She nodded and I knocked and went in. His briefcase was in his hands. "Got a coat, Tracy? I thought we'd go for a short run." He smiled. "In my car."

"Where to, Mr. Hardwick?"

"Oh, nowhere special. I've got to be home fairly early, so we can't go far."

We left the building by the main entrance. "Are you collecting Colin?" I asked.

"No. He's gone to a friend's house to tea."

We drove along the main road in a westerly direction. I relaxed and watched the countryside rolling away into the distance. Here and there an ugly slagheap disfigured the green of the fields. We passed a disused colliery and some woods and, to my surprise, the car slowed to a stop.

He braked and left the engine ticking over. "Come on, Tracy. You're going to drive."

72

I became rigid with resistance. "I couldn't do that, Mr. Hardwick. Not your car."

"I've heard that before. So often, in fact, that the next time you say it, I'll – I'll. . . ." He swivelled round and put his hands to my throat. Instinctively my hands went up to cover his and try to prise them off. Then an extraordinary thing happened. My hands became still, and I found I was actually pressing his fingers closer. I wanted him to hold me and never stop. I raised my eyes to his and wanted the world to end. I had given away my deepest longings to a man who cared not a jot about me except as father to daughter, and looked upon me as some irresponsible child who needed a paternal figure to protect and guide her.

Madly I clawed at his fingers and when he saw what I was trying to do, he removed them at once. I put my hands to my throat where his had been and we were silent. I couldn't look at him, I didn't dare.

"Tracy," he seemed to have some difficulty in speaking, "you will drive."

"Yes, Mr. Hardwick," I agreed meekly, and we changed places.

He flung himself into the passenger seat and growled, "And for God's sake stop 'Mr. Hardwicking' me. I get sick and tired of deference. We're not at school now. Go on, drive."

I released the handbrake, then pulled it back. What was I doing sitting here in the driving seat of the headmaster's car? "Why, Brett?" I asked. I had to know the answer.

He slumped back in the seat and for some reason sounded terribly irritable. "Because, my sweet Tracy, I want to give you the opportunity of feeling what it's like to drive a real car – not a heap of junk on four tired wheels. A lot of your driving trouble could be due to the fact that you've only ever driven worn-out, fourth-hand vehicles which should have been thrown on the scrap heap long ago." He looked at me at last. "Am I right?"

I nodded. "But, Brett, I'm terrified, after what happened this morning. Suppose I –

"You won't."

"But I –"

"*Drive*, woman," he shouted, "and stop driving me mad with your uncertainty and self-doubt!"

I drove. And it was a wonderful experience to be handling controls which worked, watching dials which functioned with accuracy, to be handling a steering wheel which responded to the slightest touch.

"It's fabulous," I cried, as we cruised along the main road. "It's unbelievable. It's a super car, Brett. How fast can I go?"

"Oh, put your foot down, woman. Don't be afraid. If I'm not, why should you be? It's de-restricted here, so get the feel of driving at speed."

I did. My heart sang as we sped along; it sang of the joys of living, of sitting by the side of the man I loved. The thought struck me so obliquely and sharply that my confidence wavered, and my foot on the accelerator eased upwards. Brett looked at me, but said nothing. I slowed to a less exciting pace and my energy flagged.

"Carry on, Tracy. What's the matter? What happened back there?"

"Nothing, Brett, nothing. Will you take over now?"

"All right, check in your mirror, and pull in to the side. Had enough?"

I nodded. "It was wonderful while it lasted, Brett. Thanks for giving me the chance of driving your car."

We settled into our seats and Brett drove on. He seemed preoccupied, immersed in his thoughts, perhaps even regretting bringing me out with him. I supposed we would turn round and go back now.

But Brett was driving like a man who knew where he was going. The hills rose and fell away in shallow satisfying curves, and as we rounded a bend, I saw that we were approaching some extensive woodland.

He slowed to a crawl and bumped off the road on to the level verge. "Here we are. We'll walk, and I'll talk."

He locked the car and we found a pathway through the trees and crunched over the twigs and dead leaves, picking our way carefully over tree roots. Even the birds seemed to know it was April. Their song roused me into life again, and I smiled up at Brett who was walking silently by my side, until I forced him to smile back.

"How's your hand?" he asked, and I'm sure it was only for something to say. "I've been meaning to ask." He lifted it and touched the plaster gently. "Are you looking after it?"

"It's still a bit painful, but it's beginning to heal already."

I tried to take my hand away, but he lowered it between us and held my fingers. "Tracy," he sounded as though he had at last found the courage to tell me something, "I have an apology to make, a sincere and abject apology."

We slowed to a standstill and he turned me round to face him. He looked so tall and I barely reached his shoulders. Against the background of the blue and gold above the tree tops, his face was in shade and the interwoven leaves on the branches over our heads cast a shadow over his expression. "I spoke to you so harshly yesterday morning, Tracy, so unjustly about that vicious rumour concerning us, that I hardly know how to undo the damage I must have done to your opinion of me."

I shook my head. "Whatever I felt about you yesterday, Brett, has been rubbed out by your kindness to me this morning. And this afternoon. I'm sure now that I was not to blame for that rumour. I don't know who was, but I'd do anything I could to wipe out the effect it could have on your position."

"Thank you for that, Tracy."

I don't know what it was about that golden afternoon. It must have had some magic about it, because I'm sure Brett was going to kiss me. He stared at my lips and I swear he began to lower his mouth towards mine. Then he checked himself and I decided I must have imagined it all.

We walked on, hands touching, and he spoke again. He seemed to have to force the words out. "When I got home last night, I asked my son, quite casually, if he had heard any of the tales which were going round about you and me. He said he hadn't heard any tales, no, but," he gripped my fingers, "he had talked about us to a lot of people himself."

I drew in a breath and began to speak, but he said, "Just listen, Tracy, let me do the talking." He paused, then went on, "He had told his friends and they had told their parents, and the parents had told their friends. And so the rumour grew – the rumour which eventually got back to us grossly twisted and almost unrecognisable."

I was aghast. "But what had he told them, Brett?"

"He had told them, Tracy, that you and I were getting married soon. That he had seen you that night on the moors in my arms and we were kissing each other and that, to him, could mean only one thing – I was going to marry you."

I snapped my fingers. "Of course, he asked to go outside. He saw us then. But, Brett, we weren't –"

"Kissing, no, Tracy. But in the darkness and the mist, his imagination embroidered on what he did see." His voice hardened. "I'm determined to put matters right for your sake, Tracy, as well as mine. I'm going to make him tell the truth. In public."

"But how, Brett?"

"How? I'll tell you how. He's going to come on to the platform during assembly, tomorrow morning, and deny every word he has said. He will tell the entire school the truth – that he made the story up. And then he will apologise."

"But, Brett, you can't do that. He's your own son."

"It wouldn't matter if he were the son of the chairman of the education committee. He would still have to do it. My son or not, he has to learn that he can't spread scandal and lies and start rumours as he did, and get away with it unpunished."

"But, Brett," I had to plead his son's case, "Colin is sensitive. He would never get over such a punishment. He'd remember it all his life."

His expression tightened. I tried again.

"When he saw us together, Brett, could you blame him for thinking what he did? You and I knew there was nothing in it – how could there be? – but a boy –" I paused for the right words, desperately searching in my mind for reasons and excuses, "without a mother, who's probably forgotten he ever had one –" Brett made an impatient sound, but I refused to be intimidated, "is perhaps subconsciously looking for a mother-figure, and clinging to anything that might give him hope that one day you, his father, will provide him with one."

"You, a mother-figure? Don't make me laugh. You're talking rubbish, and you know it."

I had to try again. "I don't know it, Brett, neither do you. How can we know what goes on in his mind? I can only draw on my own experiences. I went around for years envying girls whose parents were happily married."

He was quite unmoved by my pleading. "Tomorrow morning," he was speaking to himself, not me, "he will go on that platform and explain and apologise."

"Have you told him, Brett?" He nodded. "What did he say?"

"Nothing. He cried."

"Cried? Oh, Brett, how could you?"

I could see by his eyes I was getting nowhere. We turned and walked back towards the car. I could have sworn the birds had stopped singing, or perhaps I couldn't hear them for the clamour in my head. I tried once more, playing what instinct told me was my trump card.

"You're his father, Brett. He won't blame you. You're all

77

he's got. Don't forget I was the other person involved. I'm the one he'll blame, not you. He won't ever forgive *me* for the humiliation he'll suffer. And he'll hold it against me for the rest of his life." It didn't occur to me then, as it did later, that Colin would not know me for the rest of his life.

His father didn't notice my error, either. I seemed at last, and by some miracle, to have struck a responsive chord. His voice softened. "You, Tracy? How could he blame you?" The doubt was obvious, I could hear it, but had I won the battle?

We were silent after that. The sun had disappeared. The blue up there had gone, too, hidden behind greyness that promised rain.

As we drove away from those woods, I formed a plan. It was desperate, but its effect on that rumour would be deadly and final. I told Brett as we reached the edge of the town.

"Plan? What plan?"

"I can't tell you, Brett, until I know for certain that it will be acceptable."

"To whom, may I ask?"

I ignored his coldness, and closed my lips.

He looked at his watch and increased his speed a little.

"Are you late, Brett?"

"Yes. I'm taking Elaine out to dinner in celebration of her birthday."

"Oh." I shrugged away my low spirits. I had known it was hopeless from the beginning, but I couldn't stop loving him now I had started. I couldn't turn it off like a tap just because he did not love me back.

He drove through the school gates. I opened the door of his car as the sound of the engine died away.

"Thank you for the outing, Brett, and for trusting me to drive your car." I tried to smile, but it wouldn't come. I put my right hand on his arm and he stared down at it. "Will you give my – my plan a chance to work, Brett, before you – put any more pressure on Colin? Please, Brett?"

He turned my hand palm upwards and lightly stroked the plaster, then he put it from him. He said with decision, "I'll give you a day or two, no more." He switched on the ignition and waited patiently for me to get out. "Take care on the roads, Tracy."

I waved as he drove away, but he did not wave back.

That afternoon I took my car to the local garage to have the bumper straightened and the radiator put right.

After lunch next day, I found Wayne in the staff room reading the notice board. "Staff meeting," he was saying, "Monday afternoon." He beckoned to me. "Read that, Tracy. That's a good sign. The first of many staff meetings, I hope."

I read it and nodded, then I said, "Wayne, I'd like to talk to you. Could you spare the time to come and see me this evening at my digs?"

His eyes opened wide. "Unused as I am to receiving such invitations from young ladies, especially this one – yes, Tracy, I can spare the time. What's it all about?"

"Tell you when you come." I looked quickly round the room, noted it was empty and reached up and pecked his cheek.

His eyes opened wider. He took a deep breath and said, "If that's a foretaste of what's going to happen this evening, then roll on this evening!" he called after my fast-retreating figure.

He arrived when I was starting on my second batch of homework-marking. I put it aside thankfully and let him in. I had begun to feel nervous about asking him my extraordinary request. I offered him some chocolate and he pulled me on to his knee.

His mouth was bulging, and when he had finished munching, he looked at me expectantly.

I traced the line of his nose and bumped my finger over his lips to the point of his chin. "Wayne. . . ."

"When you've finished assessing my handsome profile as a

79

possible subject for a piece of sculpture, what do you want, Miss Johns?"

I sighed as I looked at him. "It's a great pity I don't love you," I said. "It would be so much easier."

He winced at my frankness. "How you do boost a man's ego! You want something, that's obvious. What would be much easier?"

"What I want, Wayne," I slipped off his knee, "is something that's going to ask an awful lot of you. I'm going to ask you – please don't be angry and please say 'no' if you must – to become engaged to me."

His mouth fell open. "To what, Tracy? You must be out of your mind. Are you seriously asking me to marry you?"

"No, Wayne, you've misunderstood. I don't want you to marry me, just to become engaged to me, for a few weeks. But the whole point of this exercise would be to make as much noise about it as possible."

He mopped his brow. "Whew, you had me worried! Just explain, only explain, that's all I ask."

So I explained and he listened. He dropped his brash manner and the real Wayne that I saw at last was a far nicer person than the one that usually showed itself to the world.

He put his arm round me and stroked my cheek with his finger. "So it's to be all holds barred, Tracy? Suppose I – er – made things awkward for you and started behaving like an engaged man?"

"Oh, that would be all right in public, Wayne, in fact it's just what I would want. But in private, no. I've told you why."

"And my feelings? What about them, my pet?"

I grinned, "You haven't got any, have you?"

"That, sweetie, is a very provocative statement. If you want me to keep my distance, don't say things like that." He became thoughtful. "So you want me to help you drag Brett Hardwick's reputation from the gutter, is that it?"

"Mine, too, Wayne. Don't forget I was involved."

"He ought to keep better control over that kid of his."

"Don't be like that, Wayne. I told you how he was going to punish him."

"Yes, he's a hard devil. I recall how he used to lord it over us when he was head of geography. Supercilious blighter, always putting me in my place."

"I never saw much of him then. He used to treat me as if I didn't exist."

"And yet you still want to help him?"

I said softly, "It's different now, Wayne."

He must have seen the dreamy look in my eye, because he said, "Don't tell me you've fallen for the man?"

I hesitated, then nodded.

He looked concerned. "But, sweetie, you're playing a losing game. I told you before, it's common knowledge that if he marries again, it will be to his housekeeper."

"It's no use, Wayne. It's a fact, I love him, and there's nothing I can do about it. I don't expect any return, especially from him. He's said the most uncomplimentary things about me," it was silly, but my eyes filled with tears, "to my face. He said. . . ."

"Don't cry, pet, I can't stand it." He stroked my hair. "Unrequited love's the very devil, isn't it? Especially for a little thing like you." He mopped my cheeks. "You know," he considered me, "anyone who could resist your tears must not only have a heart of stone, but have had it surgically removed, together with the guts of his feelings. They'd move any man –"

"Except one." I wiped away the last tear and returned his handkerchief. "Guess who?"

"Hardwick? You've cried in front of him? When?"

"When I cut my hand on the broken bulb inside his globe. He told me to pull myself together and walked out."

Wayne's fingers tightened on my arm. He made a grating sound with his teeth. "I knew he could be an unfeeling brute,

81

but that's the limit!"

"Wayne," I fiddled with the pen in his top pocket, "what shall we do about a – a ring?"

"You're really serious about this engagement business?" I nodded. "Well, I've been thinking about that – a friend of mine was engaged and the girl broke it off and gave him back his ring. If he's still got it, he might lend it to me. That would solve the ring problem."

He stood up and walked about the room. "There's only one snag, Tracy. I hope you don't mind my mentioning it, but that girl, Dinah – to be frank, I'm hooked on her. What's my position going to be when she finds out what's happened between us?"

I rushed in to reassure him. "Don't worry about that, Wayne. I'll tell her the truth – that you're doing this to help me, and there's really nothing in it. She'll understand." He looked doubtful. I went on, "I'd go and tell her now, but she's out." I felt I had to warn him. "She's got a lot of boy-friends, Wayne."

"M'm, so you said. That could be difficult."

I grinned, "May the best man win!"

He brushed his fist under my chin. "You've just got yourself engaged to me and you're wishing me luck with another woman. Odd sort of fiancée you are." He touched my lips with his. "I'll contact Bill about that ring and let you have it. All right?"

"You're really good, Wayne. How can I repay you?"

"Well, I'll consider it and let you know. A new car wouldn't come amiss."

He waved and went home.

He caught me outside a classroom next afternoon and told me he had the ring in his pocket. "When can I deliver same? This evening?"

"I'm free, Wayne, so come any time."

When he arrived, Dinah was with me. I had invited her

82

specially to show her that there was truly nothing in this so-called engagement. She was lounging in my armchair, her long legs stretched over the hearthrug, and she didn't change her position when Wayne walked in. She assumed an indolent attitude, and her fourth cigarette was half finished. She didn't usually chain-smoke, but for some reason this evening she was doing just that.

She raised her eyebrows and smiled at Wayne, and he seemed a bit puzzled by her casual manner. He was a bit nettled too, I think, and started paying me a lot of attention. He produced the ring – it had a central white stone and an imitation sapphire on each side.

"It's not genuine, pet," he told me, and slipped it on my engagement finger. "Does it fit?"

"Perfectly, thanks."

"How does it feel to be an engaged woman, Tracy?" Dinah drawled, releasing a cloud of smoke and flicking ash into the coal bucket. "I was engaged once. It's so long ago, I've forgotten the feeling."

Wayne raised his eyebrows. "And who was the lucky – or perhaps I should say unlucky – man?"

She shrugged. "I've forgotten that, too."

I frowned at her, trying to tell her to snap out of it. She didn't usually act like this. She threw away her cigarette, got up and stretched. "I've got work to do. I'll leave you two love-birds. I never did like playing gooseberry."

"Dinah, don't be an ass. I told you there's nothing in this."

Wayne turned quickly and kissed me full on the lips. "Now, having kissed the bride that is not to be, I'm going to kiss the non-bride's best friend." He walked towards Dinah, his head slightly bent, his arms rigid at his sides. Dinah tensed and they stood there staring at each other for what seemed hours. Then his arms went round her and she fell against him as if she needed the support of his body to keep her upright.

I had to get out of that room. I ran across to Dinah's place and closed the door. If they felt like that about each other, then what was I doing tying Wayne to me under false pretences, even for a short time? On the other hand, I argued, trying to rationalise things, this so-called engagement might even help things along between them – it might put them sufficiently out of each other's reach to have the effect of bringing them together.

Wayne called out a little later that he was leaving. I waved him off and met Dinah on the landing. Her eyes were shining and she had obviously been convinced beyond doubt that our engagement would be as false and short-lived as any engagement on record.

The effect of that ring on my finger next morning was really something. I met Wayne at the main entrance.

"Let's really get them talking, pet," he said, putting his arm round my waist. We pushed through the crowd of boys going to their classrooms before assembly. Staring eyes and turning heads followed our progress to the staff room door.

"That," I whispered to Wayne, "will do very nicely as a little tit-bit to tell their parents, which is just what I wanted. Now for the others."

Wayne really did the thing properly. He pulled me through the door, closed it and took me in his arms. His kiss was genuine enough, and those present audibly gasped.

Jenny came up to us, eyes like car headlamps. "What's all this, you two?" I showed her the ring. "No! I didn't think you cared!"

"Nor did I," Wayne said wickedly, winking at me, "until – until. . . ."

Surely he wasn't going to let me down? I panicked as he hesitated, "Until the day before yesterday," he finished.

Dr. Winsor shook our hands, Mike Smith patted us on the back and made the crack that he hoped our love would never "wane". In fact, everyone we met that day seemed very happy for us. My right hand, which was recovering from the cut, was beginning to feel sore again from the hand-shakings it received.

I don't think it percolated through to Brett until later. I was preparing to take a class in the geography room when Colin, who had been sitting quietly watching me as I shuffled through my folders came to my desk. He pointed to the ring and his eyes brightened.

He came close to my ear and whispered, "Are you going to marry my dad, after all?"

It hurt me to have to shake my head, hurt me to see the disappointment dull his eyes. "No, Colin."

"Who, then?"

"It's Mr. Eastwood's ring, Colin." At least I had told him the partial truth.

"Mr. *Eastwood*? But why him?"

I smiled, trying to placate him. "Why not? Don't you like him?"

He shrugged. "My dad said – oh, it doesn't matter."

He slouched back to his seat and sat kicking the legs of his chair. I quietened the class and began my lesson. Then Colin started. He rolled pieces of paper between his fingers and started flicking them across the room with his ruler. He turned and talked to the boys around him, he put paper-clips and sweet wrappings down the neck of the boy in front of him.

I had to reprimand him half a dozen times and each time it made him worse. I was shocked at his behaviour. He was usually the best behaved in the class. The others joined in and the class became uncontrollable. The uproar was deafening. I had never experienced this problem before, and I didn't know how to deal with it.

I shouted, I reprimanded, I cajoled. I talked to them in their own terms, told them to "shut up" and "belt up" in the most unladylike manner.

The door was thrust open and the headmaster walked in.

CHAPTER V

THERE was instant silence. The headmaster looked at me. He must have noted my flushed face and desperate look.

"Having trouble, Miss Johns?" he asked silkily.

There was no need to answer, he could see for himself, but I had to say something, because he was the boss. "Yes, Mr. Hardwick. I'm afraid it's just one of those days, Mr. Hardwick."

He came towards me and a folder went sprawling to the ground and landed at his feet. I bent down and as I stretched out my left hand to retrieve it, I felt his eyes dwelling on the ring on my engagement finger. When I straightened, his eyes were on my face. They were narrowed and piercing. And angry.

He turned to the class and made a few cutting remarks about their behaviour, threatened prolonged detentions if it did not improve.

"Carry on, Miss Johns. You should manage to keep them under control now." He said it as if he doubted very much that I would.

He didn't go out as I had expected, but went into the storeroom and half-closed the door. I was sure he'd gone in there to listen in on my lesson. I was sure he was doing it for the purpose.

I got agitated, felt my teeth on edge, hesitated and made foolish and unforgivable mistakes in the contour map of northern Britain which I was drawing on the blackboard. The boys shouted corrections and I thought that any moment the headmaster would walk out of that store-room, take the chalk from my fingers and tell me to sit with the boys and learn something from him.

He didn't, though, and by the end of the afternoon I was dropping with fatigue, worn out with nervous tension and thoroughly disgusted with myself. When all the boys had gone, I wondered if I should go too, but a sharp voice called me into the store-room.

My legs were dragging as I went in and stood in front of him, feeling like a criminal about to be tried for a terrible crime.

But the particular crime he had in mind was a different one. I never knew that eyes could be as cold as his as they slid from my face to my left hand hanging limply at my side.

"I take it that it's you and Wayne Eastwood I have to congratulate?"

I lifted my hand and looked at the ring. "You can if you like, but it would be a little out of place."

"I'm not sure I understand. Please explain."

I gathered up a few words in my mind and tried to put them into coherent order. Did I have to tell him? Couldn't he guess?

Apparently he did. "This is surely not your so-called plan?" He sounded incredulous. I nodded. "But how did it come about?"

"It was a bit difficult, but I asked Wayne if –"

"Don't tell me you asked him to *marry* you?"

I blushed at the thought. "Well, not really. I explained what I was trying to do – to put all the nasty-minded councillors and parents off the scent – and asked if he – would mind – becoming – engaged to me. I thought that might – solve the problem, and clear your name." I faltered under that keen gaze. "So you see, it's not a genuine engagement."

"And Eastwood encouraged you in this crazy scheme, agreed to everything you asked with no tinge of conscience, nothing? Then he's an even bigger heel than I took him to be. And he's had the cheek to apply for the headship of the geography department!"

87

I couldn't let that pass. "But, Brett, you shouldn't allow this to prejudice you against him. He's not a heel. How can you say that? He agreed to do it for my sake, to help me."

"You're in love with him." It was not a question, but an astonished statement of fact.

I couldn't let that pass, either. "I'm not in love with him. I'm in love with – I'm not in love with anybody. I told you once before, I don't believe in love."

He smiled cynically. "Before I change the subject to more important – and serious – matters, I wish to tell you that I've reconsidered my decision concerning my son's punishment. Your powers of persuasion have proved too strong for me to resist, and against my better judgement I've decided to let him off."

I tried to put my gratitude into my eyes. "Oh, Brett, thank you!"

"Why should you be thanking me? He's my son, not yours." He turned away. "I'm afraid, Miss Johns," he emphasised my surname, putting me firmly back in my place as a very junior member of his staff, "I have discovered a grave error committed by someone in this department. Tell me, who is supposed to be in charge of the films hired to show to the school geography society every Monday lunch-time?"

"I am, Mr. Hardwick. Why?"

He faced me, leaned back on his elbows against the wide shelf, and shook his head sadly. "I thought as much." I didn't like the narrow look in his eyes and grew afraid. What had I done now?

"I've had a letter – a rather nasty letter – from the firm that supplies them. It appears that one of the films we have borrowed is nearly three weeks overdue."

I covered my mouth with my fingers. "I'm terribly sorry. I must have forgotten all about it."

"Yes. And you'll be sorrier still when I tell you that this firm is so anxious to retrieve their films from hirers for further distribution that they impose on the offender a fine of around four pounds a day. I repeat, *four pounds a day,* Miss Johns."

I was appalled, shook my head. "That I didn't know. I'm sorry."

"Why not? You should have made it your business to know, Miss Johns. You handle the films, it's your responsibility entirely."

I fiddled with the ring on my finger. I could find absolutely nothing to say in my own defence.

"Have you done your arithmetic yet, Miss Johns? That is, assuming you can do multiplication. Four pounds a day for seventeen days? Have you found the staggering answer? The sum we now owe the firm concerned?"

"All that money?" I whispered. "But that's awful!"

He shook his head again. "What are we to do with you, Miss Johns?"

I began to hate my name. My heart was screwed into a tiny paper ball about to be flicked across the room. "What do you mean, Mr. Hardwick?"

He sighed. "What do I mean? I mean that I begin to wonder if you should be a teacher at all."

Someone came into the classroom and called my name. Mr. Hardwick said quietly, "Your fiancé, Miss Johns. Do you wish to talk to him?"

"No, thank you."

We were silent and after a few seconds, Wayne must have gone.

"Mr. Hardwick, everyone makes mistakes."

"Granted, but you make so many, Miss Johns."

"But how does it reflect on my abilities as a teacher if I'm unable to drive a car straight, or I accidentally knock a globe from the shelf to the floor?"

"And make shocking basic errors in front of a class, so obvious that the boys notice and have to correct you? And can't keep a class in order –"

"But that was because –" I stopped. I couldn't tell him it was his own son who started it. And why.

"And forget to return films and clock up pounds in fines?"

"But there are perfectly valid explanations for all those mistakes," I wailed.

"It's not so much the things you do – or don't do," I could see he was trying to be gentle, "as the apparent lack of a sense of responsibility which underlies them all. I would point out that I'm speaking to you officially and formally, Miss Johns. I'm speaking as your headmaster, now, not as your friend."

Friend? It warmed my heart just a little to know that he regarded me as a friend, but the warmth cooled fast when I started to get the message behind his words.

I said, in a hushed voice, "Are you telling me in a roundabout way to get out of teaching altogether? Or even to look for another job and relieve you of my embarrassing presence in the school?"

He picked up a globe-shaped pencil sharpener from the shelf, tossed it up and down in his palm. "The answer to that must be supplied by you, not by me."

"But surely, if I applied for a job in another school, they'd ask you for a reference on me. How could you give me a good reference if you think so badly of me?"

He shrugged, tossed the globe up and down, up and down. It was no use. I was shattered by the things he was saying, and I couldn't hold back those tears any longer. I could feel my confidence, never very strong at the best of times, ebbing slowly, slowly away.

"I kept telling you not to trust me, Mr. Hardwick," I said in a voice deep with tears. "Now you know why."

There was a long silence and I sobbed into my handkerchief, not daring to look at him. He spoke in a voice I could hardly hear. "My sweet Tracy, I –" He stopped. "Hell, what's the use?"

I looked up, puzzled by his sudden vehemence. He had

90

moved to the window and was staring out.

"I'll pay the fine, Mr Hardwick. It was my fault, so I must take the — the responsibility. And the punishment."

"And how do you intend to scrape up the necessary money, may I ask?"

"With my holiday savings."

He made an impatient movement. "Don't be silly."

"I'm being perfectly sensible. I've said I'll pay and I will." I dried my tears, but it was a waste of time, because more and more came. My sobs must have irritated him because he snapped, "It's quite obvious we shall have to terminate this interview. Discussion is impossible in the circumstances." He flung the miniature world on to the shelf and it bounced off, rolled across the floor and split in half. He walked out.

Then I howled. I rested my arms and my head on the shelf where his elbow had been resting and cried myself dry. So, by Wayne's definition, the heart and the feelings of the headmaster had been surgically removed, cut out and thrown away, and nothing humane or human was left inside him. How did I know that? Because my tears had left him completely unmoved.

Wayne found me ten minutes later trying to pack the film into a neat bundle. When I explained, he pushed me aside and finished the job.

"The things he said to me, Wayne. He as good as told me to get out of the school, and to get out of teaching."

Wayne jerked the string sharply, caught his fingers in a knot he was tying and uttered a loud curse. "I'd like to tell *him* to get out, but fast. . ."

He snipped the ends of the string neatly. "Get your coat. We're taking this to the post office and then I'm buying you a drink. The pubs should be open soon."

His arm was round my waist all the way to the entrance doors, and as we passed through them, Brett Hardwick came out of his room and followed us down the steps. I told Wayne who was behind us, and he said, "Right. Here goes." He pulled me round to face him, tucked the film securely under his arm, and kissed me long and passionately. I tried to pull away, but he wouldn't have it.

Brett passed us, slammed into his car and roared off down the long drive. We pulled apart and Wayne snarled, "I wonder how long it is since he's done that to a woman. So long probably he's forgotten how. I don't know what makes that man tick. Certainly not the spark of human kindness."

We posted the parcel and went to a pub. It was bright with lights. Table lamps with red shades stood on every table and a row of tiny multi-coloured bulbs was strung across the bar. It raised my spirits just to be sitting there in that scarlet glow. Wayne bought drinks and we toasted our "engagement".

"We could make it real, sweetie."

"We couldn't, Wayne, now could we? What about Dinah?"

"Ah, yes, Dinah."

"Let's drink to her, Wayne."

"With all my heart, Tracy." We drank.

"I'll tell her that, Wayne."

"Do, pet. I'd be delighted."

"Better still, tell her yourself. You could come round tomorrow evening. It's Saturday, so I'll be busy in the afternoon, and Dinah'll be out shopping. But I'm sure she'll be in in the evening."

"I might, Tracy. I might do that."

"Our 'engagement' doesn't apply at weekends, Wayne, so you're a free, unattached man on Saturdays and Sundays."

We laughed at the absurdity of it all, and he took me home.

I got up late next morning, because it was Saturday. I'd decided not to tell Dinah that Wayne might be coming. She would probably go out if she knew. She could be perverse like that sometimes.

I collected my car from the garage. It was back to its normal appearance again, although the radiator still had a slightly battered look.

After lunch, I had a hair-washing session. Then I decided to clean the windows. I put on my oldest clothes – a woollen-mixture sweater which had withdrawn introspectively more and more into itself each time I had washed it, and it now clung almost neurotically to my figure, and a pair of ancient trousers which were tight even round my twenty-three-inch waist.

It was about three o'clock and I was making myself an early cup of tea, when there was a tap at my door.

"Wayne's early," I thought, as I padded across in my bare feet to open it. How it was that I didn't fall down in a dead faint, I'll never know. There were two figures standing there – a boy, and a tall, good-looking man.

Colin grinned, "Hello, Miss Johns." He stared past me into my room.

His father asked, "Aren't you going to let us in, Miss Johns?" He had a queer smile on his face.

I tried to get my breath back, but I was still stupefied with shock. I couldn't speak, so I opened the door wider and let them in.

The untidiness of the place brought back my powers of speech. I apologised profusely and said I'd find some better clothes and pop over to Dinah's room and change.

"No, don't do that." Brett's eyes moving all over me riveted my feet to the ground. "You'll do just as you are."

Colin was roaming round and picking up my tiny glass ornaments and inspecting my books. I was still confused by the whole situation, and remembered with an effort my duties as a hostess.

"Do sit down, Brett." I dived across to the armchair and removed the clothes that were draped across the back, plumped up the one cushion and said I hoped it was comfortable. I asked him if he'd like a cup of tea, and he said, please, he'd

93

love one, and so would Colin.

So I plugged in the electric kettle and filled the teapot, and still I felt too shy to speak to him. It was just as well Colin was chatty because the silence would have been a very long one otherwise.

He poked about and tried to find my bed, and I told him I slept on the armchair which opened out into a bed. He told his father to stand up so that he could try it out, but Brett refused to move.

"Run away and play, Colin," he told him impatiently. "I want to talk to Miss Johns."

"Have you told her why we're here, Dad?"

"You know very well I haven't had the chance. You've been doing all the talking since we came."

"Sorry, Dad. Haven't you got a kitchen, Miss Johns?"

"No, Colin. This room's all I've got. It's a bit cramped and I get a claustrophobic feeling at times, but it could be worse."

I glanced shyly at Brett and saw that he was watching me. He seemed to be wearing old clothes himself. His tweedy jacket was patched with leather at the elbows and the knife-edged creases were missing from his trousers. He didn't look in the least like the smart, efficient executive-type he looked at school. But I liked him much better this way. He was so much more human and approachable. Almost as though he possessed feelings – and a heart.

I poured the tea and handed him a cup. He refused the sugar, but Colin tipped three teaspoons into his.

"I didn't tell you I was coming, Tracy," his father was saying, "because I knew you'd tell me not to. You said once before that you would never invite me here."

"Why, doesn't she like you, Dad?"

"Shut up, Colin." Colin laughed. "He's a pest sometimes," his father said, under his breath.

"Well, you had me, Dad. It's your fault I'm here."

Brett cleared his throat and looked intensely embarrassed.

94

It was the first time I'd ever seen him like that. It made me want to throw my arms round his neck, so I moved away quickly.

"Colin," I said, "I've got an atlas here that's my pride and joy. It's very big and very up-to-date. Have a look at it. It cost me a lot of money, so take care of it."

I pulled it from the shelf and opened it out on the floor. Brett came to crouch down beside me and looked at it, too. He admired it and looked at me enquiringly.

"I saved up for it," I explained. "It took me months."

"With a lovely book like this, Miss Johns," Colin gave me an impish look, "I don't understand how you can make so many mistakes at school."

"Colin!" His father's reprimand made him look up quickly.

I swallowed the lump in my throat and shook my head. "It's all right, Brett. It doesn't matter. The last time he said it you laughed, remember. I suppose he thought it was good for a laugh this time."

"Don't sound so bitter, Tracy."

"Whose fault is it if I do?" The words were out before I could stop them. "Anyway, can you now tell me why you came?"

"I've – er – come to give your car that servicing I promised it. I saw it standing in the drive. Would the landlord object if I tackled the job there?"

"No, he doesn't seem to mind what we do. As long as we're reasonable, he's reasonable."

"Right." He stood up. "I'll get the toolbag from my car, and make a start."

"It's very good of you, Brett, especially after. . . ."

"That's all right. It's my housekeeper's weekend off and she's taken her son to stay with relatives. I was at a loose end, so I came. Hope you don't mind entertaining my son."

When Brett had gone, I took the crockery downstairs to wash it in the kitchen we all shared, and while I was there

95

I thought with a shock that I'd have to invite them both to tea. After all, servicing a car was a long job . . . but what about food?

I raced up the stairs to inspect my stores. I was short of bread, and had only enough milk to see me through till the morning. Dinah. I must get her help. I told Colin where I was going and hoped Dinah had returned from shopping. She had. I threw myself on to her chair and told her all.

She reeled backwards with surprise. "So that's who it was with his head in your bonnet? If you know what I mean? So that's Brett Hardwick. He's quite a dish, my dear. He smiled at me as I passed, and being female, my curiosity was aroused. He's surely not the ogre you've been telling me about?"

"He is, Dinah. He changes his spots. I've never seen him so human, so – ordinary." I couldn't tell even my best friend the things Brett Hardwick did to my heartbeats.

She let me have some ham and tea and sold me a cake she had just bought. As I carried them across to my room, Colin came out.

"Hallo," Dinah said to him. I introduced them. "I think Colin's bored, Dinah."

"Would you like to come and see my equipment, Colin? I teach art. Do you like art?"

"Well, I'm not very good at it, but. . . ."

"Come on in, lad." Dinah pushed him through her door and turned to me. "I hope you'll do the same for me one day, dear."

I laughed and thanked her. It was time I issued that invitation to Brett. I ran down the stairs and into the drive. I talked to the lower half of his body because the other half was ear-deep in the engine. He didn't hear me, so I rested my hand on his back.

He jumped as though he'd been shot. He withdrew inch by inch from the bonnet and stared at me. "Tracy, my dear, I'm sorry. I didn't know you were there." He looked like a self-conscious boy, which endeared him to me more than ever. "Actually, I was thinking about you – about you in relation to this car, I mean. It's a wonder you haven't come a cropper long ago, it was in such a state. You'll have to take more care of it from now on, you know."

"Yes, Brett," I said meekly. "I only wanted to ask if you and Colin would like to stay to tea."

He smiled. "I was hoping you'd invite us. I took a chance on it and brought some food. Do you mind?"

"Mind? Lead me to it! I've just asked Dinah to lend me some."

He wiped his hands on his handkerchief and went to his car which was parked at the kerb. He opened the boot and took out a shopping bag. "Bread, milk, eggs and a cake. I raided the fridge and the larder."

I opened the carrier bag and looked inside. "What will Elaine say when she comes back, Brett? There's an awful lot here."

He laughed. "I'll meet her wrath when I have to. I think I can handle her well enough." He studied the screwdriver in his hand in great detail. "She usually takes everything in her stride. I've never known her get worked up about anything yet."

I pondered that statement and got nowhere and said, "We'll have to have tea in my room, Brett. It's a bit cramped, but I hope you don't mind."

"You know the answer to that, Tracy." He wound himself down into the bonnet again and I went into the house. I found my best tablecloth and scraped together just enough crockery and cutlery.

The cake Brett had given me was a magnificent gâteau, filled with fresh cream and elaborately decorated with icing. I put it in the centre of the table, where it deserved to be. I made sandwiches of egg and ham and hard-boiled some more eggs on my gas-ring. When tea was ready, I sent Colin to tell his father. Brett came up the stairs trying to remove the

97

grease on his hands with his handkerchief. I was horrified and told him so. "Your poor housekeeper, how does she get your hankies clean?"

He looked surprised. "I've really no idea. What else can I use?"

I laughed at his stunned expression. "I'll give you a clean rag and some washing-up liquid and you can wash in the bathroom." I pointed to the door with frosted glass panels in it. "A bit primitive, I'm afraid, but it's better than nothing."

When he came back his hands were spotless, but his face still had one or two grease marks on it. "There's no mirror in there," he said, when I told him about them.

"Never mind. You can get them off after tea. I'll lend you a mirror."

At tea-time, Colin was in high spirits and kept the discussion going. I pulled the cake towards me.

"Pity to cut this magnificent work of art, isn't it? I suppose you want a piece, Colin?"

He looked at his father. "Shouldn't we sing 'Happy Birthday' or something, Dad?" Then his eyes opened wide and he let out a prolonged and guilty, "Oh-oh-oh!"

"Colin, you ass! I told you not to mention it."

"Birthday? Whose birthday? Yours, Colin?" I looked from one to the other.

"No, Dad's, actually."

"And no one told me? Why not?"

"Sorry, Tracy. It didn't seem important enough."

"Not important? Everyone's birthday is important."

"That's what I told him, Miss Johns."

"Of course we must sing 'Happy Birthday'." And we did, the two of us. The recipient of our good wishes looked appropriately embarrassed, and our song was followed by an expectant silence as I cut into the cake and passed the portions round.

Colin was the first to show appreciation and I soon followed with mine. Colin remarked, again to his father's embarrassment, "It was worth what you paid for it, Dad, even though it cost a lot of money."

I poured out some more tea, and as I handed Colin his second cup, he asked, "When are you coming to our house again, Miss Johns?"

"Why, would you like me to?"

"Well, you liked our model railway, didn't you, and it was a change to have a girl there instead of another boy." He started to look self-conscious and his father raised his eyebrows at me and grinned.

"Looks as if you've got yourself another boy-friend, Miss Johns."

Colin turned pink and I smiled and changed the subject quickly. "Have you finished my car, Brett?"

"Nearly. There are one or two small jobs to do, then your car should be in better running order than when you bought it. Never buy a second-hand car 'blind' again, Tracy. Always get a qualified mechanic to vet it before you part with your money."

Brett went outside to the car and Colin and I washed up in the bathroom. After that, he went back to Dinah's room to "splodge some paint on paper", as he put it.

Brett was soon back. He sprinted up the stairs and my heartbeats sprinted up the scale. "Finished," he said. "Got that rag again, Tracy? I'll wash my hands."

He came back with the grease spots still decorating his face. "Shall I get them off?" I asked shyly.

He smiled. "That's a good idea." I took the cloth from him, squeezed out a drop of detergent and raised the cloth to his cheek. I rubbed that clean, then stretched upwards to his forehead. He was so tall and I was so short, I found myself having to lean against him to reach the mark above his right eyebrow. I misjudged and hit his eyelashes. As he flinched backwards, I fell on to him. His arms came out to steady me

99

and I was looking straight into two quizzical grey eyes.

"I'm so sorry I hurt you, Brett," I breathed. "It was an –"

His lips cut off the last word from mine and his kiss was like nectar in my mouth. It was a long, long drink for both of us and we were a little drunk when it was over.

"Happy birthday, Brett," I whispered. "Are you thirty-eight now?"

He made a face and nodded. "See my grey hairs?"

I said I could, but they didn't bother me. "They don't make you old."

"No? To a little girl like you they must do."

"Little girl?" I pulled away, but he jerked me back. I resisted until I felt his breath on my lips again. My legs turned to water, I heard nightingales in my head and a loud hammering on the door.

"Tracy? Are you there? Can I come in?"

We came to our senses and pulled apart. "It's Wayne! I forgot he was coming."

At a stroke, Brett became the autocratic headmaster. "Never get your dates mixed, Miss Johns. It could be embarrassing."

Wayne grew tired of waiting for an invitation and walked in. He stared, momentarily quite out of his depth, but his unusual discomfiture lasted only a few seconds. He strolled across to me and trapped me in his arms. "Entertaining a VIP, sweetie? You might have warned me. I'd have come in my best clothes."

I struggled away from him. How could he burst in like that, when he had really come to see Dinah, not me? I was sure the ice in Brett's eyes was meant for Wayne, but somehow a coating of hoar-frost clung to me, too. "I'll collect my son and be off. Which room is he in?"

I ran across the landing to Dinah's room and called Colin. He came out reluctantly. "Are we going already, Dad? Can't we stay a bit longer?"

"No, we can't. Miss Johns' fiancé has arrived."

100

Wayne stood in my doorway and Colin grinned. "You here as well, Mr. Eastwood? Quick, Dad, before any more teachers turn up, or I'll begin to think I'm back at school. Ugh!" With that expressive sound he dived down the stairs, stopping at the bottom to call up to Dinah who had joined us on the landing. "Thanks for letting me paint, Miss Rowe. Can I come again some time?"

"Any time you like, Colin. Nice boys like you are always welcome."

I ran down the stairs after Brett, and I heard Wayne say, "What about nice boys like me, Miss Rowe? Am I welcome?"

I had to get to the car before Brett drove away. I was just in time. "Please don't go, Brett," I said, bending down and speaking across Colin, through the front passenger window, "before I've thanked you. It was so good of you to service my car."

He talked to the windscreen. "That's all right, I did it in the interests of road safety."

I wanted to make him look at me. "I hope you enjoyed your tea."

"Yes, thank you," he told the dashboard.

"And that you've had a happy birthday."

"Yes, thank you," he said to the steering wheel.

It's a good thing he didn't look at me after that, because he would have seen the tears in my eyes.

I stood back and he drove away. Only Colin turned and waved.

I trod wearily up the stairs. Wayne had disappeared. So Dinah had let him in, after all. I didn't see him again that evening. He didn't even call in to tell me he was going home, although I heard him leave just before midnight. Well, at least somebody's happy, I thought, as I heard their whispered good nights on the landing.

CHAPTER VI

I MET Wayne at lunch-time on Monday. "Tell me, Tracy," he said, putting both arms round my waist, "what was golden boy doing at your place on Saturday? Dinah said he was servicing your car, but I didn't believe her."

"That's right, he was." I grew anxious. "You haven't told anyone, have you, Wayne?"

"Not a soul, sweetie. After all, I'm supposed to be your fiancé, aren't I? Would I tell the world you'd been entertaining another man in my absence?"

"It wasn't like that, Wayne, and you know it."

"Ah, but I don't know it, do I? Are you trying to persuade me he was taking a fatherly interest? It didn't look exactly a father-daughter relationship when I butted in. The air was thick, but thick, with intrigue."

I laughed, and as Pete Green came into the room, Wayne kissed me. Pete tutted and muttered something about "love's young dream", and subsided behind a newspaper.

"By the way," Wayne caught my hand as I went to my desk, "Jenny phoned to say she couldn't make it to school to-day. She's got a foul cold, and asked if you would take the lead at the staff meeting this afternoon."

Pete Green lowered his newspaper. "Can't Jenny come? Bad luck. She's been looking forward to having a go at the head-master."

"Yes, well, our Tracy will be a good substitute, won't you?"

"Not again, Wayne. I was no good last time. We didn't get a squeak out of him, did we?"

"Ah, but things have changed between you," he corrected

102

himself quickly, "I mean us, the staff and him, since then, haven't they?"

"No, they haven't, Wayne." I hoped my voice was cold enough to freeze him, but it wasn't.

"Well, Jenny was sure you'd understand, and would do it for us. *I* can't, pet. You know why."

He didn't like to mention the departmental headship he was hoping to get in case Pete Green was listening, but I understood.

I gave in. "I suppose there's no alternative, then. I'll have to do it. He's got a low enough opinion of my work already. It can't go any lower, whether I do it or not."

Wayne patted me on the back. "Good girl."

I was not looking forward to the staff meeting. I wondered how Brett would act – would he be the high and mighty headmaster, or would he let his human side show?

It didn't take more than a few moments to discover the answer. He was the high and mighty headmaster. As he came into the staff room, his eyes flicked towards me, taking in the way Wayne was sitting with his arm across the back of my chair, playing the attentive lover.

I met the headmaster's eyes for a fraction of a second and shivered. The room suddenly felt cold. He took his place at a table in the centre of the semi-circle of chairs and glanced round to see who was there. I was holding Jenny's notes and knew it was only a matter of time before I would have to speak.

Brett began, "I have called this staff meeting – I intend it to be the first of many – to discuss a number of queries which have arisen since my appointment as head teacher of this school." He spoke about certain routine matters, then went on to discuss the changes suggested by the "committee for action."

He held their list in his hand. "You will appreciate that changes like these will take time and money. The time factor will no doubt tax your patience and the money required to

103

make these alterations will tax your pockets, as ratepayers.

"The new equipment for the science laboratories and the installation of a language laboratory in the English department, both of which I agree with, would have to be considered by the governing body of the school. The ideas would then have to be submitted to the education committee and so on. Time and money both involved.

"Now, car parking facilities for staff. There is little I can do about that, I'm afraid."

This was where I felt I had to go into action. I put up my hand to catch his attention and tried to control my rapid heartbeats. I took his raised eyebrows as an invitation to speak.

"Mr. Hardwick, the action committee wishes me to point out," I read from Jenny's notes, "that cars are parked at present on part of the playground. We think this is a dangerous practice. We suggest that part of the extensive lawns in front of the school could be torn up and the area then concreted for the parking of staff cars."

There was a heavy silence as he considered my words. When at last he spoke, his words were clipped. "Miss Johns, you must surely realise that the lawns and flower beds you are speaking of are the sacred cows of the councillors. The front of this school was landscaped immediately after the building was completed, and is the pride and joy, not only of the local authority, but of the parents whose boys attend this school. It would be beyond my powers, and my sphere of influence, even to mouth such a sacrilegious suggestion."

"But, Mr. Hardwick, you don't have to park your car there. You don't realise how dangerous and difficult it is to manoeuvre a car in between boys kicking footballs round and fighting, and trying not to hit them."

He gave me a withering look and I curled up into the protection of Wayne's arm. I had let myself be carried away more than I had intended.

"You, Miss Johns, are no doubt too young to know that I

104

was once an ordinary member of staff at this school. I remember, with perfect clarity, undimmed by my advancing years, that I too had to manoeuvre my car day after day between groups of boys fighting and playing. There is no need for you to spell out the dangers for my benefit. Whatever you may think, I am not yet so old that my memory is failing."

There was a tittering amongst the teachers and their expressions were scandalised as they looked at the object he had lashed with his sarcastic tongue. Wayne's arm moved protectively round my waist. But now I had started, I wasn't going to be quelled by the headmaster's sarcasm.

"In that case, Mr. Hardwick," I answered back, "you'll realise how we feel every time we drive into these boys playing, quite legitimately, in their concreted playing area. They aren't the ones at fault. Legally, we are. What would happen if we knocked any of them down? We would be responsible as motorists, not you or the governing body."

"Miss Johns," Brett's eyes were glinting angrily, "it is not within my jurisdiction to give any pronouncement on the legal position, if any unfortunate accident were to happen. And if *I* don't know, I fail to see how *you* can claim to know. Such a matter would have to be referred to the local authority's legal adviser."

I shrugged despondently and subsided into my corner. He had won on points. He gave me a last piercing look and went on to the next subject.

"Gym changing rooms need to be altered." He frowned. "I'm not sure what that means. Can anyone enlighten me?" He looked expectantly at Pete Green, but Pete shook his head and looked pointedly at me. So I was the lamb to be slaughtered again, was I?

I read from the notes, "The existing changing rooms are filled with stores and pupils have to change in the corridor. We suggest that this matter be looked into without delay."

"May I ask whose notes you are reading out, Miss Johns?"

105

"They're – they're Miss Willis's. She's away ill and asked me to speak for her."

"I see." He fiddled with some papers, then asked, "Isn't there anyone else present who could act as spokesman, someone who is more experienced in these matters, and would have a more mature and reasoned approach to these subjects?"

Again there was a horrified hush, and I actually felt sick at his words. How could he talk about me so unfairly in front of my colleagues, and cast doubts so openly on my integrity?

The silence was deep enough to touch. Pete Green said at last, "Since Miss Johns has been nominated as our spokesman, the majority of us are quite satisfied, and have every confidence in her powers of persuasion."

I wanted to get up and throw my arms round Pete's neck. Someone at last had stood up for me. Not even Wayne had done that.

But Brett looked even blacker as he listened to Pete's remarks. What was wrong with what Pete had said? The changing rooms were quickly dealt with. He said he sympathised with the teacher in charge, but felt that little could be done at present to remedy the matter. It was mainly a question of finance, he said, always a difficult subject.

He looked round the room. "Any more queries?"

I waved Jenny's notes. "Yes, Mr. Hardwick. There's a mention here of some suggestions and complaints made by some of the older boys. One of them is the provision of a properly equipped sixth form common room, with armchairs and table tennis equipment –" He cut me off sharply.

"These are matters which I shall deal with myself, after consultation with the head boy. There is no need for you to elaborate further." Again, he had cut me down to size, and I wilted visibly.

Wayne leaned sideways and kissed my cheek. "Well done," he said loudly. Brett lampooned us with his eyes, and declared the meeting closed.

106

Everyone stood up as the headmaster walked to the door, but I hadn't finished with Brett Hardwick yet. I called out, to the astonishment of the staff, who obviously thought I must have had enough of the rough side of the head's tongue for that day, "Mr. Hardwick, may I see you for a few moments?"

He came to an abrupt halt at the sound of my voice, looked at his watch and said, "You have exactly ten minutes. If the business you wish to see me about can be done with in that time, yes, you can see me. If not, then I'm afraid it will have to wait."

"It will take two minutes, Mr. Hardwick."

He walked out as if he hadn't heard. They all crowded round and congratulated me on my stand. Grasping my handbag, I pushed my way through them to the door. I knew that if I hung about too long, reaction would set in and I would either start crying or shaking. And I knew also that the crumbs of courage I had so painstakingly swept into a neat pile inside me would be scattered to the winds.

I tapped on the headmaster's door and entered at his bidding. He was standing at his desk and looking down at some papers. He glanced up briefly. "Yes, Miss Johns?" It was almost as though he wanted to avoid my eyes.

I think he was expecting me to refer to the way he had spoken to me at the meeting, but I had too much pride to do so. I felt inside my handbag and produced a piece of paper which I put in front of him. He picked it up and frowned.

"What's this for?"

I had to steady my voice. I could feel reaction catching up with me fast. "It's a cheque, Mr. Hardwick, you can see that. It's my first contribution towards the payment of the fine on that film."

His eyes opened wide. "But this is a lot of money. Where did you get it from?"

"I didn't steal it, Mr. Hardwick, if that's what you think."

My voice shook. "It's the money I've put aside monthly to-wards my summer holiday. I told you before that I would use it to pay the fine." I looked round for a chair. "I'll pay the rest in instalments at the end of each month." My legs felt weak. I had to sit down. "I'm sorry," I managed to say, "I feel a bit funny." I sat down, and my teeth started chattering. "I'm sorry," was all I could say. "I'm sorry."

Then he was standing in front of me. "Tracy," he said, so gently I wanted to cry, "I wondered where all your Dutch courage came from. It doesn't do, you know, to get so emo-tional about things. You're not made of the right stuff to stand up to the cut and thrust of public debate. I've told you that before."

He walked to a cupboard and took out his coat. He draped it round my shoulders.

"You n-needn't have spoken to me l-like that. You n-needn't have said those n-nasty things about m-me."

He crouched down and looked into my face. "They shouldn't have chosen you, Tracy. They should have had your courage, your tenacity, and spoken instead. *They* didn't have the cour-age to stand up to me as you did. They didn't even give you any support."

"Except one."

"Except one, but even he was cowardly in the way he re-ferred me to you, even though it was his own subject." He took my hand, but I drew it away. "I admire you for your courage, Tracy, more than I can say."

The shaking subsided slowly. "It's nice to hear you say something p-pleasant about me," I said. "You say such awful things sometimes."

He laughed, he actually threw back his head and laughed.

"Perhaps," I went on, "they think I've got some influence where you're concerned. How wrong they are!" He laughed again. I began to feel happier. I smiled at him.

"That's better," he commented. "There's colour in your

cheeks now. You looked like a ghost when you came in."

He removed his coat from my shoulders and put it over a chair. There was a tap at the door and he called "Come in." I stood up to go, but he stopped me. "It's Elaine."

She came in and was surprised to see me. "Hallo, Miss Johns."

"Good afternoon, Mrs. Langley," I answered, and Brett said, "For goodness' sake drop the formality. It's Elaine and Tracy."

We smiled at each other, and I saw how charming she looked without her glasses. She must have taken to wearing contact lenses at Brett's insistence. Perhaps he had even paid for them. She was wearing a pale pink lightweight two-piece which went well with her blonde colouring. Her sandals, handbag and gloves were white and she looked as cool and collected after a day's shopping as she must have done after a good night's sleep. She hadn't a hair out of place and she made me over-conscious of my flushed cheeks and my humdrum outfit – dark-blue skirt and orthodox white button-up blouse.

Her shopping bags were bulging and she sighed and sank down into Brett's chair. "My feet are killing me," she moaned.

He smiled indulgently. "Well, it looks as if your efforts were not in vain. Did you get everything we wanted?" He turned to me. "I let Elaine have the car today. She dropped Colin and me at the school this morning and now she's come to take us home."

"Yes, I'm not just your housekeeper, Brett, I'm your chauffeur, too. I'll have to demand an increase in wages."

They were smiling at each other as Brett told her, "If you asked me nicely, you might even get it."

I was clenching my fists so hard, my nails started to dig into my palms.

"Anyway, I got what I wanted for both of us," Elaine said. They were talking like an old married couple even before the ring was on her finger.

"I bought myself a dress," Elaine went on, "and got you two shirts, one sober and one rather gay – I hope the collar size is right," she mentioned a size and he nodded, "two pairs of socks and two pairs of –"

He stopped her quickly. "Don't go into details about the next items. I know exactly what you're going to say." He looked at me. "We have a very young lady with us."

There he goes again, I thought. Little girl, very young lady. Good God, I'm an adult, a woman – hasn't he got eyes?

I stood up. "I must go. Good-bye, Elaine."

"Good-bye, Tracy. Nice to see you again. I hear you had a bad hand?"

"It's better, thanks. I now have a rather spectacular scar, but I'm told that will go."

Brett came to the door. "About that cheque, Tracy – if I accept it, does it mean you'll have to do without your summer holiday?"

"Yes, but you must accept it. I insist. It was my fault. You've told me I've got to act more responsibly, and this is my way of doing so."

He shook his head, lost for words, and ruffled my hair as though I were a child. I walked away from him feeling about two feet high.

I didn't see Wayne next day until the evening, when he came unexpectedly to see me. "Dinah's out," I informed him as soon as he arrived.

"Is she? Oh. Well, it's you I came to see."

"That makes a nice change, having a visit from my fiancé."

He laughed and dropped a kiss on my cheek. "I want to ask you something." He sat down and tugged me on to his knee. "How long do you intend our – er – engagement to go on, Tracy?"

"Why, do you want to break it off already?"

110

He laughed again. "What a question to put to your husband-to-be!"

Those words sounded so final I frowned. "You're not, though, are you?"

"No, I'm not, pet, so you can take that frown off your face." He looked me over. "All the same, you're an appealing little thing, aren't you, with your soft hair and big blue eyes. No wonder golden boy is so taken with you."

"Don't be silly, Wayne. Everyone knows he's going to marry Elaine. And judging by the intimate details they were discussing yesterday afternoon in his study, it won't be long, either."

"Be your age, pet. A man can be engaged to one woman but still have eyes for another, especially one like you. And what was he doing when you went to his room after the meeting? Kissing you better? And stop looking so self-righteous. After the way he spoke to you at the staff meeting, I thought he might have had a small twinge of conscience. Come on, tell uncle, did he kiss you better?"

I slipped off his knee. "It's no business of yours."

"It is. I'm your fiancé."

"If you're going on like this, Wayne, I think we'd better end this arrangement." I started to take off the ring.

"No, no, pet, keep it on. For my sake, as well as yours."

"For your sake?"

"Yes." He looked uneasy. "It's Dinah, Tracy. She's an awkward little cuss."

"Is she being difficult? I warned you she had lots of boy-friends. But how does it help your cause if we stay engaged?"

"Well, I thought it might – just – make her jealous."

"So you want me to play up to you, now? But, Wayne, she's my best friend."

"I know I'm asking a lot of you, Tracy, but it shouldn't be for long. A few more weeks?"

I thought about it. "We'll give it to the end of term. Will that do?"

"Thanks a lot, Tracy." He went home soon after that.

A few days later, I had a summons from the headmaster. Would I go to his study at morning break?

"Sit down, Miss Johns." He motioned me to a chair and continued with his writing.

I fiddled with my handbag strap and wondered what was coming. I didn't have long to wait. He placed his pen on his blotter, leaned back and looked at me closely. I smoothed my hair, thinking it was out of place. I twisted the top button of my blouse, I recrossed my legs. I wished he would get on with it.

He picked up a letter. "With regard to that overdue film, Miss Johns, I wrote to the firm concerned, explaining the position fully. I made all the excuses I could think of on your behalf, and it was a letter which would have broken the heart of the hardest-headed business man." He smiled briefly. "They have replied, informing me that the film is now to hand, and in view of the circumstances described in my letter, they are prepared to reduce the fine to a quarter of the amount due." I was about to say that the cheque I had given him would cover that, when he stopped me. "I haven't finished. I've thought about the matter, and I can't have any member of my staff, I don't care who it is, going without his or her holiday as a form of punishment for committing what was, after all, a very human error, so I've decided to pay the fine out of the school funds."

"Oh, but, Mr. Hardwick, that's hardly fair to the boys."

"Will you be quiet, Miss Johns? I have therefore written you out a cheque for the same amount as the one you wrote out to me, and I insist that you accept it."

"But, Mr. Hardwick —"

He interrupted quietly. "I will not have you play the martyr, Miss Johns. You will accept this cheque, or else," his eyelids flickered and his voice grew soft, "I shall be very tempted to put you across my knee." He held out the cheque.

112

"Now will you take it?"

I took it like a lamb. "It's very kind of you, Mr. Hardwick."

"Kindness doesn't enter into it, Miss Johns." He changed his tone. "But talking of being kind, and harking back to holidays, tell me, are you going away next week?"

"For half-term? Yes, I'm going south to visit my mother." I told him where she lived.

"Are you going alone or with your fiancé?"

"He's not my —" I stopped. I was part of the act now, I had to support Wayne. "Alone. Wayne's made other arrangements."

"I see. You're surely not intending to drive yourself all that way?"

"No." I laughed. "I think my car would fall to bits if I drove it such a long distance. It would probably sit down in a lay-by and refuse to budge another inch, like a donkey."

He laughed, picked up a pencil and doodled a very good outline of the British Isles on his blotter. "I was wondering whether Colin and I could offer you a lift."

"A lift, Mr. Hardwick?"

"Yes, a lift, Miss Johns. My sister lives near Stevenage and we're spending the week with her and her husband. I usually go south via the A1. It's a straightforward journey. We stop for lunch about half-way, and I aim to arrive mid-afternoon. If you came with us, you could call in and have a cup of tea and meet my sister. Then I'd run you to the local station and you could catch the London train from there."

"It's very kind of you, Mr. Hardwick, but —"

"Now don't give me that old one, 'oh, I couldn't, Mr. Hardwick'. Our relationship passed beyond that stage weeks ago. And for heaven's sake, stop Mr. Hardwicking me." He thumped on the desk. "Now, are you or aren't you accepting my offer?"

"Well, I —"

"You are. Right. I'll have a word with you nearer the time

113

and make final arrangements. Now," he glanced at the clock on his wall, "I'm going to have my coffee and you've got a few minutes left to have yours."

We smiled at each other as he showed me out.

For the rest of the week I was wrapped in a cocoon of ecstasy, a secret delight that bordered on rapture.

Wayne stepped up his evening visits. Sometimes Dinah was with me and Wayne was exaggeratedly attentive and loving towards me. I played up to him because I'd promised I would, but I didn't like it. I think he was trying to get a reaction from Dinah. She reacted all right, but in the wrong way. She boycotted me, almost stopped being my friend. When I told Wayne, he said it was a good sign — it showed she was jealous, but, knowing Dinah, I wasn't so sure. I hoped things would work out between them while I was away at half-term.

I told Wayne I was getting a lift from Brett, and he laughed. "My, my, we're getting as thick as thieves, aren't we? Watch out, he'll be making improper suggestions next!"

That annoyed me. "I keep telling you, it's not like that. He's just —"

"Taking a fatherly interest, I know. Don't give me that nonsense any more, pet. It sticks in my throat."

But he could say what he liked, nothing could alter the fact that I was going south with Brett and his son. In fact, I'd barter the rest of my half-term holiday for those few hours in Brett's car.

On Thursday morning, he called me into his room to fix a time for him to pick me up. Mid-morning, he suggested.

"Coffee-time," I said.

And at coffee-time, they came. We had two cups each and I washed up while Brett stowed my case in the boot of his car. I was as excited as a small child, and he must have noticed it, because he said, "I feel like a benevolent uncle who's taking his favourite niece for a birthday outing."

114

I looked down at my clothes. I was wearing slacks and a long, chunky-knit, button-up jacket. "I hope you don't mind if I wear these," I said, pointing to my trousers. "They're more comfortable to travel in."

"Mind? Why should I mind having an attractive young woman sitting at my side?"

Colin moaned, as we got in the car, "Why can't I sit in front, Dad? I usually do."

"He can sit here if he wants, Brett. I don't mind."

He grew impatient. "I want you here," he said, tapping the seat next to him, "and here you'll sit. Colin will have to get used to the idea."

"What does that mean, Dad? You going to marry Miss Johns after all?"

There was a stiff silence and I could see Brett was angry. I cut off his shout by turning to Colin. "I can't marry two men, Colin." I waved my ring about. "I'm engaged, remember."

"Oh, yes. To old Eastwood. Why him? My dad's better than him."

The car jerked as Brett did a bad gear change. "Anyway, Colin," something made me go on, "your father can't marry two women, either."

Brett asked icily, "What is that supposed to mean?"

"Your – your housekeeper. Everyone knows you're going to –"

Colin roared with laughter. "You don't mean he's going to marry old Elaine?"

I couldn't stop the shout this time. His father was so furious, I knew it must be true. "Colin, *shut up!*" It was a command which would have made anyone but a member of the family want to slink away and hide. I had a sneaking feeling the remark was meant for me as well as his son, so, not being a member of the family, I shut up fast.

The atmosphere between us improved as the miles passed.

115

I offered again to let Colin sit in front, but Brett was adamant. I thought he was being hard on the boy, but it was not my place to say so.

I passed some of the time trying to work out why he wanted me beside him. He didn't need a map reader because the route was a straight line between two points, with only slight variations. He didn't want companionship because he didn't talk much. He left that to his son. By the time we stopped for lunch, I had given up the riddle.

We had a good meal in a rather expensive restaurant. When I offered to pay my share, Brett quelled me with a look, and I wanted to slide under the table.

We got back into the car, and Colin rolled about holding his stomach saying he had eaten too much. That didn't please his father, either. I couldn't understand why he seemed so on edge.

He asked about my visit to my mother. "Will she mind you arriving late?"

I shook my head, trying to visualise my mother's face. It was difficult, although I kept her photograph in my handbag. I hadn't seen her for almost a year, because there hadn't been room for me to share Christmas with them. Dinah had taken pity on me and asked me to her party.

"I won't even be staying in her house. She's got her husband's parents staying there," I couldn't bring myself to call him my stepfather somehow, "and I'll have to sleep next door."

"I see." He sounded a bit grim.

"What's your sister like, Brett?" I asked shyly.

"Vivienne? Well, although she's my sister," his son sniggered at his father's words, "she's very pleasant. We get on well together and you'll like her. My brother-in-law's an executive working for a chemical firm. Comfortably off, big house, all the mod. cons. you could wish for."

"Sounds nice." I sighed, thinking of my mother's cramped old semi-detached house in a shabby suburb of London.

116

"When are you and Mr. Eastwood getting married, Miss Johns?"

Colin's question caught me below the belt. In fact, it floored me. I got up, dusted my thoughts down and replied, "We – we – well, really there's nothing definite yet." I changed the subject rapidly. "I think, Colin, it's time you stopped calling me Miss Johns and called me Tracy. Don't you think so?" I appealed to his father.

The answer put me back on the floor. "No, I do not think so. I can't think of any reason why he should stop calling you Miss Johns."

I was slapped down, put firmly where I belonged, outside the family circle, and there I must be content to stay. I bit my lip and subsided into my corner. After that I didn't want to talk. I could feel a headache coming on, and I tried to ward it off by relaxing my muscles one by one. But it was no use. I sensed a tension in Brett's body as he sat rigidly concentrating on the road ahead, and it had communicated itself to me.

We were twenty or so miles from the end of our journey, when he pulled into a lay-by. "Would you take over for a while, Tracy? It would give you some practice in motorway driving."

"I'd rather not, Brett, I've –" He didn't give me a chance to tell him about the persistent pain which was by now a sitting tenant in my head, and resisting all my efforts to evict it.

He turned on his headmaster's voice. "I want you to drive, please. I'm not asking you, I'm telling you. If you're afraid, which is what I suspect, it will force you to face your problems and not run away from them."

I looked at him appealingly. "Please, Brett, I'd rather not. Couldn't you just have a rest and –"

Without another word he edged himself out of the car and walked round to me. "Get out, Tracy." There was no arguing with that authoritative voice. I got out. I got in the other side. The sooner we were moving off, the sooner the ordeal would be over. I started the engine, released the handbrake and looked over my right shoulder to choose the correct moment to move out into the stream of traffic.

"Wait, Tracy." Brett's hand was on my knee. "Before you go, fasten your safety belt."

I shook my head, already committed to moving out on to the motorway. "It doesn't matter, Brett. I won't be driving long, will I?"

He hissed something under his breath and I caught the words, "Obstinate little fool!"

I pretended I hadn't heard. As I became accustomed to the strong pull of the engine, I settled down and began to enjoy the sensation of driving a quality car. Sometimes I pushed my foot down on the accelerator too hard and we spurted forward alarmingly, then Brett would caution me and I'd ease off a little. If it hadn't been for my headache, which was getting worse, I would have given in to the urge to pull out into the fast lane and put my foot down really hard.

"You're doing well, Tracy." Brett's praise made me light-headed. "Keep it up. We're nearly there."

We reached the outskirts of the town and he directed me through the side roads and main streets. "At this junction, go straight on. Don't turn right."

I noticed that the car some way in front was taking up the correct position on the crown of the road to make a right turn, so I pulled over to the left to overtake it and carry straight on. As I approached the nearside of the car waiting to turn right, I sensed that something was wrong. Too late I realised I was going much too fast and had misjudged the width of the space between the other car and the kerb.

A fraction of a second before I could jam on the brakes, we hit the rear of the other car. There was a sickening thud and the other car slewed sideways across the road. We were flung forward and a thousand hammering pains joined the other pain in my head. I didn't lose consciousness, but I wished

I had. The pain was almost more than I could bear.

"My God, she's done it again." Those familiar words swam round and round in my head like aimless goldfish. I think I rolled sideways towards the door. I could feel it cold against my neck and then hands pulled me back, shaking fingers tugged at the buttons on my jacket. "Oh, God, Tracy, Tracy," the words came over and over again.

"Is she all right, Dad? She's bleeding, Dad." The agitated voice from somewhere behind me made me try to surface and focus.

"Brett, I'm sorry," the words sounded odd and my lips were annoyingly lazy. "I'm sorry, I'm sorry." I couldn't think of anything else to say. I didn't want to open my eyes, I didn't want to see the damage I'd done. I was lifted out in someone's arms, the noise of a siren shrieked and screamed blue murder at the hammers in my head. Someone was dabbing at my forehead and I didn't think it was Brett. It had to be Brett. I called out his name, and he answered, "I'm here, Tracy, I'm holding you, my dear." I tried to open my eyes to see his face, but my eyelids refused to work.

In the end I gave up and just lay still. I wanted to sleep. There seemed to be dozens of people around, but I had to sleep. So I turned my face away from them all and slid into sweet unconsciousness.

CHAPTER VII

I SEEMED to be struggling. Someone was undressing me and someone was washing me. Strong arms lifted me and lowered me gently into bed. I had no desire to open my eyes. The effort would have been too much. Voices were all around my ears and I tried to listen, but the words were jumbled. A hand was holding my wrist. The voices grew quieter and ceased altogether. A door was shut. I shut off my mind and drifted into sleep.

I awoke next morning to a terrible feeling of failure and a doctor holding my wrist. I ached all over. A hundred pneumatic drills were boring holes through my skull.

"Hallo, young lady. Come to join us?" I couldn't smile back. I didn't think I could ever smile again. Brett was in the room and a woman I had never seen before. The doctor placed my hand on the bed cover.

"Mild concussion, a few days in bed."

I shut my eyes until they had gone, then I looked round. A spare bedroom, with striped wallpaper which, had my vision been normal, would have pleased me but which, at that moment, offended me.

The curtains were flowered and blowing gently in the breeze. The sun seemed to be shining outside the window. The small dressing-table was littered with my belongings. I was too lethargic to look further. Someone came in and curiosity aroused me from my apathy and made me see who it was.

Brett's gentle smile was more than I could bear. I turned my head away. He sat on the bed, took my hand. I tried to think of something to say. The only thing I could manage was, "I'm sorry, Brett, but I had a headache."

"Why on earth didn't you tell me?"

"I tried. You wouldn't listen. And even if I had, you would have said I was putting it on." Why did I feel so full of resentment, instead of contrition? I thought about the damage I must have done to his car, and became repentant. "I misjudged the width, I was going too fast. I'm sorry."

He stroked my hand. "You weren't used to the dimensions of my car." He bent down and whispered, "And you should have *worn the safety belt!*"

I couldn't stop my lip trembling. "I know that – now." Then I asked, "Your car – was it badly damaged?"

He shrugged. He had obviously decided not to tell me the truth. "The engine worked. I drove you here in it. Then I took it to a garage near here. They said it would take about four days to put right."

"The car I hit?"

"A nasty dent in its rear. It could have been worse. The insurance companies will have to sort things out between them."

"It looks as though you're all right, Brett."

"The safety belt saved me. You got injured because you were thrown forward and your head hit the windscreen." He looked at the dressing on my forehead. "Does it hurt?"

I wanted to say it felt as though a football crowd was trampling on it. "Not too bad. It was very kind of your sister to take me in. She looks a nice person." I stared inside the bedclothes. "I'm wearing my nightdress. Who –?"

He walked to the window and stared out. "Vivienne undressed you. I helped." I was glad he couldn't see my face. "I phoned your mother, Tracy. I got her number through directory enquiries. I explained and she sent her love. I told her you would be here for a day or two and gave her our phone number in case she wants to enquire how you are."

I thanked him. "I can't impose on your sister for too long.

121

I must make the effort and get to my mother's somehow."

"Not before you're ready, Tracy." He stood by the bed, and lifted my left hand. "What about your fiancé? Do you want me to let him know what's happened?"

"No, no, thanks. Anyway, I've no idea where he is, and even if I had, I wouldn't want you to contact him."

"I understand, of course. You don't want him worried."

I didn't understand what he was getting at. I was about to tell him that nothing would worry Wayne where I was concerned, but drew back. I had told him often enough that our engagement was false, but obviously he hadn't believed me, so what was the use?

"I'll call my sister."

She came in, a tall, graceful woman in her mid-forties, her brown hair interwoven with grey. Her eyes were like her brother's, except that hers were warm and compassionate, whereas his were usually withdrawn and cold.

I thanked her for all she had done. She said she was sorry she'd had to do it.

"Perhaps I can get up soon?"

Brett was emphatic about that. "You'll stay where you are, my girl. Doctor's orders."

"But —"

"No buts."

Vivienne laughed. "He's putting on the headmaster act, Tracy. Don't you stand for it. You're not at the school now, you're on holiday. But you must rest, my dear. A day or two in bed, that's all, then you'll be fit enough to travel. Are you dying to see your parents?"

I looked quickly at Brett.

"They're divorced," he said briefly.

"Oh, forgive me, Tracy. I had no idea. . . ."

I tried to sit up. My limbs were aching and made strong objections to the movement. Brett stooped down and lifted me under the arms, and held me upright while Vivienne plumped

122

up the pillows. He took his hands away slowly and I tried to recover from the feel of him.

"I must look a mess," I said.

"You couldn't," Brett said, smiling.

"You might feel a mess, my dear, but no, you don't look it. Perhaps you'd feel better if I combed your hair?"

She found my comb and ran it through my tangled hair. "There now, she looks very nice, doesn't she, Brett?"

"Beautiful," he said obediently.

"Now, breakfast. What would you like?" Vivienne asked.

"Oh, nothing much, thank you. I'm not very hungry."

"Well, I'll send you in a tray, and you must eat what you can."

Colin put his head round the door. "Can I come in?" He stared at me. "Are you all right, Miss Johns? You look awful."

I had to laugh, especially when Brett pretended to throttle his son. "Here we are trying to build up her morale, and you send it flying with one swipe!"

"You look fine, Colin. No damage, no cuts and bruises?"

He shook his head. "I had my feet up behind Dad and when we stopped my legs bent and I shot forward and hit my bottom," he put his hand behind him, "on the seat in front."

"So he gave himself a good hiding," his aunt commented.

I laughed again.

"See, Dad, I'm cheering her up."

Brett took his son by the collar and marched him out.

"I'll get your breakfast," said Vivienne.

Brett brought it in. It was set attractively on a tray, and he made me eat every bit. It was wonderful just having him sit there and talk. When Vivienne came in for the tray she asked me if I would like a wash. "We must make you look pretty. You have an admirer, Tracy. My son is dying to meet you."

"You've got a son?" I visualised another Colin, perhaps a year or two older.

123

"Yes. He saw you brought in yesterday dead, as he calls it. Now he wants to see what you look like alive."

Brett went out of the room and left us talking. "I'll bring a bowl and soap, Tracy," Vivienne said.

I told her I could go into the bathroom, but she insisted that I stayed where I was for the moment. "Later, perhaps, if you feel you can manage it."

I washed and looked in my compact mirror, and hated what I saw. The dressing was larger than I thought, and stretched for some way across my forehead. It was too much effort to put on any make-up. My arms felt heavy and it was a relief to sink back into the pillows and just lie there inert.

I went over recent events in my mind and that feeling of helpless dejection caught up with me. I loved Brett, but he didn't love me. He loved Elaine. I was engaged to Wayne, but he didn't love me. He loved Dinah. That little calculation left me right out in the cold, and in the cold I was likely to stay.

I drifted into a light sleep and awoke suddenly, becoming conscious of voices. The bowl of water had gone. Someone must have crept in and removed it. The voices came from another bedroom, and although they were speaking quietly, the two people had not bothered to close the door, thinking, probably, that I was still asleep.

"She's wearing an engagement ring, Brett. You didn't tell me in your letter. Who's she engaged to?"

"A chap called Eastwood, a member of staff at school. She told me once it wasn't genuine, Vivienne, and I can't get to the bottom of it. They behave at school as though they're madly in love, yet every time I mention his name, she shies away like a frightened horse."

"She seems so young, Brett. She's such a little thing."

"Vivienne, she's a babe in arms. She's so —"

"Sh–sh!" Someone must have crept on to the landing, then returned to the bedroom. "I thought I heard Colin. Let's shut the door."

So I was a babe in arms now. I remembered all the words Brett had used about me — a very young lady, a little girl, a child, now a babe. I was going backwards in time, getting younger instead of older. I turned my head restlessly from side to side, hoping to stem the tears, but they came relentlessly, sliding down my cheeks to my mouth.

"Tracy! My sweet Tracy, why are you crying?" Brett sat beside me, held my shoulders. I turned away. I nearly cried out, "I'm not your sweet Tracy. Talk to Elaine like that, not to me."

He tried to pull my head foward to his shoulder, but I pulled away. He stood up abruptly, and changed his tone. "Stop crying, Tracy. Tears won't help, they'll only hinder your progress."

His astringent tone made me worse, and I started to sob. He walked up and down the room. He went out and Vivienne came in.

She dried my eyes and stroked my hair. "If I don't pull myself together," I thought, "she'll begin to believe her brother when he calls me a child." Gradually I quietened down, and she gave me my handbag.

"I expect you feel better for that, Tracy, don't you?" I nodded. "Now put on a bit of make-up and you'll feel better still. You need cheering up. I'll send Colin in. By the time he's finished, you'll feel as cheery as Santa Claus."

Colin came in, but he wasn't alone. He brought a stranger with him, a tall young man with dark hair and grey eyes. "This is Robert. Robert, here's Miss Johns. She doesn't look dead now, does she?"

Robert laughed. "She looks very much alive, Colin. How do you do, Miss Johns? I'm — well, I'm one of my mother's twin sons. Is that clear? Colin's my cousin and —"

"Dad's his uncle," Colin finished.

He was uncannily like his uncle, too, with the same look in his eyes and Brett's quiet authority in his manner.

"I understand you need cheering up. We've been given strict instructions to make you laugh."

"One look at Robert, and that's enough to make anyone laugh." Colin dodged as his cousin lunged at him.

I laughed at them, and Colin said, "There, she's laughing already! I'll go and tell Dad. He told me to let him know how we got on."

"You do that, pal. And forget to come back."

Colin made a face and left us.

Robert and I looked at each other, and I laughed again. "It's funny," I said, "but when your mother spoke about 'her son', I visualised another Colin, only perhaps two years older."

Robert pretended to be indignant. "Let me tell you, Miss Johns, that I'm ten years older than my little cousin."

"I see that now. So you're about my age, then?"

"Now that tells me how old you are. Thanks."

I felt at home with him already. "You — you haven't said it yet."

"Said what?"

"That I look young for my age. Don't you see me as a child, like everybody else?"

"Child? Good gracious, no. Very — er — grown up, if I may say so." He sat on a chair. "Do I have to go on calling you Miss Johns, like Colin?"

"Please make it Tracy, Robert." He was inspecting his nails very closely, so I asked him, "Where's this twin brother you mentioned?"

"Clive? At his home a few miles away. He's married, has a young son."

"Married?" I was astonished.

"M'm. That puts things in a different perspective, doesn't it?"

I wasn't sure what he meant, but I went on, "So that makes you an uncle and Brett —"

"A great-uncle, yes."

My heart sank. That placed Brett in a different generation.

Robert was still inspecting his nails. "You – you're engaged, Tracy?"

I looked at my ring. "Yes and no, Robert. Really, no."

"That, if I may say so, is as clear as mud."

I laughed. "Sorry about that, but I'll try again. It's not a real engagement. We both agreed to it for different reasons, for our own special reasons. We'll be breaking it off at the end of term, but don't tell anyone, will you? Otherwise the whole object of the exercise will be lost."

He seemed to brighten. "Cross my heart and so on, Tracy, I'll keep it strictly to myself."

"Thanks, Robert." There was a friendly silence until Robert asked, "You like folk music, Tracy? I've got a few good recordings. If you can stand it, I'll bring in my record player and you can hear them."

"I'd love that, Robert. I often wish I had one myself, but I haven't been able to scrape enough cash together since I bought my car."

"My uncle's got one. Ask him if you could borrow his. He never listens to music now, although he used to once upon a time."

"I don't think I could do that." I shrank at the thought. Borrow something of Brett's and give it back ruined?

"I'll ask him if you like."

"No, no, thanks, Robert. I wouldn't have time to listen anyway."

He went out and returned with records and record player.

"Some of the songs are sad. You won't want to hear those, will you? It'll be more than my life's worth if they find you crying again!"

He played some of my favourites. No one else came in.

"My uncle must have put Colin on a leash," Robert commented. "Otherwise he would have been back and making a pest of himself."

We were laughing when Brett walked in. His eyes went from me to Robert and back and he strolled over to the bed.

"You look better already." He looked down at me. "It seems as though my nephew is good medicine."

"You can buy me over the counter at any good chemist's, without prescription," said Robert. "By the way, Uncle, Tracy wants to borrow your record player."

I blushed violently. "No, I don't, of course I don't."

Brett looked at me speculatively. "Now which of you do I believe?"

"Me, Uncle. She's too shy to ask. She said she couldn't afford to buy one."

"I haven't any records, so what would be the use? Anyway, I'd only break it, like I break everything else."

"Hearts as well, Tracy?" Robert asked casually.

"I'm not the heartbreaking type. Nobody's ever fallen in love with me yet, and I don't suppose they ever will."

Brett walked to the window, hands in pockets.

"Nobody loves you, eh, Tracy?"

Robert inspected the stylus on his record player. "It wouldn't be difficult," he said. When I looked at him enquiringly he explained, "To fall for you."

I laughed. "Now you're flattering me, probably to make me feel better. Unless you want something?"

The two men exchanged glances. "I feel superfluous," Brett said abruptly, and walked out.

At lunch-time Robert took away his equipment and promised to come back later. Brett came in with Vivienne after lunch and watched her while she changed my dressing.

"Can I have a mirror, Vivienne? I want to see how bad it is."

"It's best if you don't, Tracy," Brett answered for her. "A day or two, perhaps. I think you should know that the doctor had to insert a few stitches. Don't look so worried, my dear.

128

It won't detract from your prettiness. He said the scar should fade completely with time. Most scars do."

I knew of one scar that would never fade. I slept for most of the afternoon, and in the evening Robert came back. I asked about his father.

"He's in Holland this week. He's a research chemist, and often has to go abroad for his firm."

"What's your job, Robert?"

"I'm studying law. It's a long time before you finally qualify. The pay's not too good in the early stages."

"Nor is a young teacher's," I told him. He asked me where I lived and he said he would suffer from claustrophobia if he had to do the same.

We were still talking when Brett and Vivienne called in to say good night. Robert left with them, and said he would be back tomorrow – without fail, he said with a smile.

"I'm glad," I told him. "I've enjoyed your company."

"Obviously the liking's mutual," Brett muttered, and went out.

The next day passed pleasantly and quietly. I had visits from most of the family, but Brett didn't stay long. He seemed off-hand and casual, and my spirits dropped again. As soon as I was fit enough to leave, I would go. I couldn't stay in this house, with his family, and with him so near and yet so far away from me.

On Tuesday morning, I told Brett firmly that I was going to get up. He tried to stop me, but I was determined.

"Anyway," I said, "I want to see what the rest of the house is like, besides this room and the bathroom!"

"You win. But you'll spend the day sitting in the lounge."

And that is what I did. Robert entertained me with his music and his conversation, Colin played the fool to make me laugh, and Vivienne waited on me. Only Brett kept his distance.

129

"I must go to my mother's on Thursday," I told them. "I'll only have three days with her, as it is."

Brett and Robert had an argument about taking me there, and Robert won because Brett thought his car would not be ready in time. I insisted that I would go by train, but nobody listened.

I packed my case the following evening, and we sat in the lounge chatting. Robert went out and Colin was sent up to bed. Vivienne asked her brother, "Are you and Elaine still hitting it off?"

"Why shouldn't we be? She's the best housekeeper I've ever had. I hope she'll stay. In fact, I'll make darned sure she does."

Yes, and I know how, I thought forlornly. The phone rang. Brett answered and called me into the hall. "Your mother," he said, smiling as he handed me the receiver. He pulled up a chair for me, obviously expecting me to be talking for some time, and went back into the lounge, leaving the door ajar.

"Hallo, Mum."

"Hallo, Tracy dear. How are you now? Feeling fit again?"

"Yes, thanks, Mum. Everyone's been very kind. How are you, Mum? It's good to hear your voice again. I'm looking forward to coming tomorrow. It seems years since I saw you."

"Yes, it is a long time, dear. I'm fine, thanks. So's Jim." (My stepfather.) "What I phoned about, Tracy, was to tell you that it's a bit awkward about your visit. When I wrote last, I thought next-door would have a bed free, but Mrs. Wilkins has got her mother-in-law come to stay without any warning. So would you feel too awful, dear, if I suggested you put your visit off a bit? Do you mind, dear?"

Of course I minded, I wanted to scream. I minded so much it hurt. My own mother doesn't want me, I wanted to shout in her ear. I had to keep down my near-hysteria and speak normally, especially as Robert had just come in the front door.

130

"You mean — not come this time? Of course I don't mind, Mum. I'll go home tomorrow instead. I've got my bag packed, so I'll catch a train north, instead of south."

"I thought you'd understand, Tracy dear. And I'm so glad to hear you're feeling better. Take care of yourself. Keep writing, won't you, dear?"

"Good-bye, Mum." I put the receiver on its cradle and stood there, staring.

"Tracy?" I turned towards Brett and stared at him.

"Yes?"

"Something wrong?"

"No. No, nothing's wrong, nothing at all. My mother said she doesn't want me to go there, that's all. There's no bed for me. So I'll go home, Brett, I'll go home tomorrow. I've got my bag packed, so I'll go home." I realised I was repeating myself, but I couldn't help it. My head started to throb and I put my hand up to try to stop it.

Brett came across the hall. "What's the matter? Are you upset?"

"Upset?" I looked at him wildly. "Why should I be upset?"

He held my elbows and looked into my eyes. The anxiety and deep compassion I saw in his for the first time brought my tears to the surface and I broke down. As he took me in his arms, I cried with the abandonment of a child.

He walked me into the lounge, which I sensed was empty, and pulled me on to the couch beside him. I clung to him because at that moment, he seemed the only stable, unchanging thing in my life, the rock to which I had to hold fast or drown.

He let me cry myself out, then he spoke. "You must stay here, Tracy, for the rest of the week and come back with us on Sunday."

I tried to refuse, said I couldn't poach on his sister's generosity any longer, but he overruled me. I borrowed his handkerchief to dry my eyes.

131

"Bed for you now, my girl. After that, it's all you're fit for."

On the landing, we stood for a moment face to face. I played with a button on his jacket and he covered my hand with his.

"Thank you, Brett, for your sympathy. I'm sorry I cried all over you, but –"

"I'm getting used to the role of rescuer of damsels in distress," he tilted my face, "especially this one. Trouble seems to follow her around like a pet poodle."

We laughed and parted.

Brett's car came back from the garage next day. We all walked round it and said how well it had been repaired. During the afternoon, Brett took Colin and Robert for a run to try it out. He came back satisfied.

"All's well," he said, answering my anxious look.

"Was it terribly expensive, Brett?"

"It was – expensive, Tracy, yes." He tapped my cheek with his finger. "And I'm not telling you how much. It's the insurance company's worry now. That's what drivers pay their premiums for."

I was sitting on the couch and relaxed into the cushions. I sighed. "That's something I won't have to worry about in the future. I've decided to sell my car."

The silence that greeted my statement was prolonged and thick. Robert, beside me, stared at his uncle like someone waiting for a time-bomb to explode. Vivienne, likewise. Brett was staring at me, and I stared back defiantly.

"You're not, you know," he said.

"Oh, but I am. Nothing will make me change my mind. I'm not driving again. I'll let my licence lapse."

"Oh no, you won't, Tracy."

"Oh, but I will. How could I drive again? Three accidents within a few weeks. You once called me a menace on the roads, and you were right. So I'm getting off the roads, fast." I challenged him. "And what's more, you can't stop me."

He came across to the couch, motioned Robert away and took his place beside me. He sat sideways, one leg draped over the other, and studied me as though I were an interesting specimen.

"So you're giving up the fight? You're letting three minor accidents, all of which can be explained away rationally, get the better of you?"

"Minor? You call the last one minor?"

"I do. Looking back on it in perspective, it was very minor." I shook my head as though he were mad, but he persisted. "Your guilt feelings, your emotions are blowing up these incidents out of all proportion."

"Brett," his sister tried to intervene, "leave the girl alone. It's her own business if she decides to give up driving. I can't say I blame her. I don't enjoy it myself."

"Her own business?" Her brother glared at her. "Is it, Vivienne?"

She sank back into her chair. So he could even quell his sister with one of his ice-cold looks.

Robert joined in. "Uncle's right. If you give into your fears now, Tracy, you'll have it on your mind all your life. The challenge you failed to meet. You'll never forgive yourself."

"All right," I shrugged, "so I'll never forgive myself. What does that matter?"

"Take it from me, Tracy," Brett stood up abruptly, "it matters. It matters a hell of a lot." He slammed the door behind him.

Next morning, Brett took me to the shops. We went in his car. Even sitting in the front passenger seat I became tense.

It was fun shopping with him, though, and he seemed to enjoy it too. We had coffee in a mock-Tudor café, and Brett had to bend his head to avoid the beams. For some reason, he was in high spirits and we laughed a lot. I tried to visualise

133

him again as he was at school, cool, detached, a little austere, then I looked at the handsome face opposite me, crinkled with laughter, and gave it up. He had two personalities locked inside one body; the one frightened me, the other filled me with inexpressible happiness.

As we drove home, he told me he was taking me for a drive during the afternoon, so after lunch we went out. Colin had wanted to come, but he had been firmly snubbed by his father. We were soon driving through the pleasant country lanes, the trees in full leaf now, and a promise of summer heavy on their boughs.

"Where are you going for your holidays this year, Tracy?" Brett asked.

"Scotland, probably. I'd like to penetrate to the northern areas. They say it's even more beautiful there than the better known parts."

"It's my ambition to go to the northern isles. It's somewhere I've never been. I'll have to remedy that one day. Which reminds me, you know there's another geography field trip fixed for the first week of the summer holidays?"

"Yes, I remember. Who – who's coming with me, Brett?"

He stared ahead and didn't answer for a few minutes. "Since no head of department has yet been appointed to take my place, I assume the deputy head will be going with you."

I tried to hide my disappointment. "Wayne?"

He nodded. "Would you like that, Tracy?"

"I – yes." My voice was flat, but he didn't seem to notice. "Will he – will Wayne get the job of department head, do you think, Brett?"

He paused before he answered. "The interview's in two weeks' time." His tone reprimanded me a little for asking him. "There are five on the short list. He is one of them." He might also have added, 'Discussion terminated. Mind your own business.'

He turned off the road into a farm gate and switched off

the engine. We sat in silence for a few moments and listened to the bird song and the country sounds. A tractor was busy in the distance, a horse whinnied, a dog barked sharply.

"Now you're going to drive, Tracy." Like a crash of thunder, his words roared round my head.

"I told you, I'll never drive again."

He repeated his words, quietly but firmly. "What's more, we're sitting here, all night if necessary, until you take this wheel and drive. I'm absolutely adamant, Tracy. Nothing will move me from my decision. So come along." He moved to open his door.

"And nothing will make me change my mind." The bravado of my words belied my fear.

"Wrong. I will make you change your mind."

I began to panic. "You can't. Remember what happened before when you forced me to drive against my will." Another awful thought struck me. "And you only got the car back yesterday. If I damaged it again, I'd – I'd want to die."

"Getting dramatic won't help. I repeat, you are going to drive. Now."

"I'd rather get out and walk." I felt for the door handle, opened the door, but his fingers caught my wrist in a punishing grip. "You can't make me, Brett. I refuse." I pulsated with fright, felt the net closing. He got out and strode round to my side.

"Out." I shook my head. "All right, if you don't mind submitting to the indignity of being lifted bodily out of this seat and deposited bodily in the driving seat, that is precisely what I shall do. My strength is infinitely greater than yours, Tracy, both of body and of mind."

I knew I was beaten and took refuge in abuse. I clenched my fists. "It's true, then, you are cruel. You haven't got a heart or feelings." He caught my arm, jerked me to my feet. I struggled. I knew I was growing hysterical. "No woman would ever stay with you. Your wife was right to call you cruel!"

The palm of his hand made contact with my cheek in a stinging slap. I stared at him, shocked back to normality. "How could you?" I whispered. "How could you?"

His eyes burned, his face was white. I had never seen him so angry. He pointed to the driving seat. "Get in." I got in. "Put on the safety belt. I've tightened it for your use."

Mechanically, I slipped it over my shoulder, clipped it round my waist. I wasn't really thinking, my brain was petrified into numbness. I sat with my fingers resting loosely round the steering wheel.

"Switch on the ignition," he said. I did. "Check for traffic." I did. "Handbrake, gears...." I did it all automatically. We pulled out on to the road, and then the numbness wore off. I was driving again and I was terrified. My eyes were playing tricks, I flinched from each vehicle that came in the opposite direction, the hedges seemed to draw me to the left like malevolent magnets. Each time a car came up behind us, I slowed down to let it overtake. I knew I was driving badly and wanted to scream, "I can't go on, I'll have to stop."

But I knew, at that moment, that I had to go on. If I stopped, I would lose my self-respect, my nerve would snap and I would be haunted in my dreams by self-reproach and failure. I drove on, and on, until the voice beside me, soft now and deep with emotion, said, "Stop, Tracy. Pull off the road on to the verge."

We bumped to a standstill. I braked and switched off. I closed my eyes, my head sagged on to my chest, my arms fell to my sides. I was physically and emotionally exhausted.

"Well done, my sweet one, well done. I knew you had courage." He pulled me towards him, but I lay limp in his arms. He kissed my cheek where he had slapped it. His mouth moved across to my lips. My head flopped back and I was as lifeless as a rag doll. He drew his mouth away, waited a moment, supported my head with his hand and tried again. I responded to his kiss no more the second time than the first.

I think in that moment I almost hated him for what he had made me do, and for trying to make amends in this way afterwards. He had already drained from me all I had to give. Now I could give him no more.

CHAPTER VIII

HE put me from him. "Move across, Tracy." His voice was cold. "I'll drive now."

I eased my way over to the other seat, closed my eyes and let my head rest on the side of the car. We did not speak a word on the way back. When he turned into the drive and switched off, he came round and opened my door. I got out, walked dazed and unsteadily towards the house. He did not attempt to help me. We went in and he called his sister.

She came into the hall, took one look at me and turned to her brother. "What have you done? Made her drive?"

"Yes. She drove. She needs reviving. Give her some brandy."

He turned and went out again. Vivienne came across to me and put her arm round my shoulders. We heard the car revving up and roaring away down the road. "My dear, you look terrible. Sit down, for goodness' sake."

I sat in the lounge and the brandy burned me into awareness. Her sympathetic eyes were upon me, and I put the empty glass on the coffee table. "You'll soon feel better. Don't let my brother get you down. He's a hard man, at times."

I was too weary to choose my words. "Is that why things went wrong with his marriage?"

"Well, to be fair, no. His wife played her part in making him that way. They should never have married. They were both too young and inexperienced."

"But your other son is married, and he's young. Aren't they happy?"

"Yes, they're very happy. So much depends on the temperament of the people involved, I suppose. I think Brett loved Olivia at first. She was beautiful enough, but brittle, cold. He was warm-natured, but as time went on he grew an armour of coldness to match hers. He told me one day, when he was at his wits' end over where their marriage was going, that Olivia just wasn't interested in the interchange of love, either mentally or physically. Because he wanted to behave towards her like a normal husband, she told everyone he was cruel. Then the baby started coming. She didn't want it, he did. She blamed the baby on his 'cruelty', as she called it."

My face burned. I remembered the things I had said to him in the car, the unforgivable accusations I'd made. And afterwards I had repulsed him, pushed him away when he had tried to make amends. And all the time, I should have been the one to apologise.

No wonder he had been angry. He was still angry when he came back. He opened the lounge door, looked at me long and coolly, and asked, "Are you feeling better?"

"Yes, thanks." I smiled, hoping for an answering warmth in him, but he was no more responsive to me than I had been to him in the car.

Vivienne came to sit beside me. Her action seemed almost protective, as if she wanted to shield me from her brother's anger.

"Don't forget you're having your stitches out tomorrow morning, Tracy. Brett, will you be taking her to the doctor's surgery?"

"I'd rather not. Couldn't you? You could use my car."

Vivienne frowned from him to me.

"Would you, Vivienne?" I asked. "I'll be glad of some moral support."

"She shouldn't need to have her hand held," her brother said sharply. "She ought to be able to stand on her own two feet."

I clasped my hands so tightly it hurt.

Vivienne shrugged his bad temper away. "Have you looked at your wound, Tracy? You must have taken a peep under the dressing?"

"No, I – I was afraid." I didn't need to look at Brett to feel his contempt at my remark. I half expected him to rip the dressing off and force me to look in a mirror and face up to yet another of my problems.

For the rest of the day, Brett ignored me. Robert took over where he had left off. He was attentive and entertaining, and I felt his mother's questioning eyes on us more than once. The more Robert waited on me, the frostier Brett became.

I played up to Robert more out of bravado than anything else. I didn't think he was serious, any more than I was. In the end, Brett walked out of the room and I didn't see him again that day.

Vivienne borrowed her brother's car to take me to the surgery. The stitches were quickly removed, and when I took out my compact in the car afterwards, I was shocked. The wound was red and jagged, and although partially healed, it was obvious the scar would take a very long time to disappear. I was sure I would have it for the rest of my life.

"You'll have to grow a fringe," Vivienne encouraged. "That would hide it well."

"I look awful with a fringe," I said childishly.

But Vivienne just laughed. So did Robert when we got back.

"I don't know what you're worrying about," he said, "it doesn't spoil your looks in the least."

"I haven't any to spoil." I knew I was being childish again, but Robert patted my back.

"Now she's fishing for compliments. All right, let's give her a good catch, shall we, Uncle?"

"Count me out," his uncle replied, and left the room.

During lunch, Robert said he was taking me for a drive.

"We'll have tea out, shall we, to celebrate your stitch-removal?"

"That's a good idea," his mother said. "Since it's her last day here, you might as well make the most of it."

I looked at Brett, but he was leaning back and staring out of the window. Then I checked myself. What was I doing, seeking his approval? Asking permission of the headmaster to go on an outing?

"It sounds marvellous, Robert. I hope the sun stays out."

It did. We drove into the countryside in Robert's ancient red sports car. Then we walked along a public footpath across the fields and sat under a tree and talked.

"Tell me, Tracy," Robert said, "what is your exact relationship with my uncle?"

It was a difficult question and I tried putting him off.

"He's my headmaster and I'm a geography teacher on his staff at school."

"Now tell me some more."

"There's no more to tell."

He frowned. "Why did he bring you here?"

"Because I was stupid enough to crash his car."

"Yes, I know that, but why did you go in his car in the first place?"

"He offered me a lift south, that's all. It's the truth, Robert. There's nothing more to it."

"But the other evening, when you were crying all over him, the way you were clinging to him for dear life, I could have sworn you were in love with him."

I had to think fast. "But, Robert, I was in such a state I would have clung to anyone at that moment. If you'd been standing next to me, I would probably have cried all over you."

He brightened. "Really? If I'd known! From now on I shall shadow you, my girl, just in case you get all worked up and want to cling to me." He held out his arms. "Try me now.

141

Just practise."

I laughed, "No, thanks. I'm quite happy at the moment."

He became serious. "I'm glad, Tracy. I'm happy in the same way."

I wanted to avoid what might happen next. I looked at my watch. "Is it tea-time yet? I'm getting hungry."

He stood immediately, held out his hand to help me up. "Tea it shall be."

We found an old house standing back from the road with "Teas" chalked on a blackboard propped against the hedge.

It was fun sharing a meal with Robert. He was so like his uncle must have been fifteen years before that I half-closed my eyes and tried to pretend Brett was sitting opposite me. Just the two of us, young, carefree and in love.

"You've drifted off, Tracy. You're sad again. You've looked sad a lot this week." He clicked his fingers in front of my eyes. "Snap out of it. Come on, let's get on our way."

When Robert unlocked the car, he paused, and looked at me. "Care to drive, Tracy?"

I saw the challenge in his eyes, saw the car, shabby, well-worn, inviting. "Might as well," I said.

So I drove that old sports car through the country lanes, on the motorway and through the crowded streets back to Robert's home. He didn't congratulate me when I braked in the drive. He just took it for granted.

We went into the house hand-in-hand and met Brett in the hall. "She's done it again, Uncle. She's driven my car. Took it up to sixty on the motorway and didn't turn a hair."

Brett's eyes rested on my face, flushed with effort and triumph, then he looked away. "Good," was all he said.

That evening, Robert and I were alone in the lounge. I was examining the bookshelves when he came across and turned me round.

"I'll miss you, darling," he said. "When will I see you again?"

142

I knew he was going to kiss me, and I didn't want to resist. Perhaps, deep down, I imagined it was Brett, and when Robert's kiss went on and on, I began to respond. We pulled apart when the door was opened, then closed slowly.

"Don't go in there, Dad," we heard, "Miss Johns is kissing Robert."

"Correction," said Robert, against my lips. "Robert's kissing Miss Johns."

The door opened again, someone stood watching us, then retreated.

"We're on show," Robert murmured.

Footsteps sprinted up the stairs and a bedroom door banged shut.

"Whoever that was obviously disapproved," I said, pulling away and sitting on the couch.

"Why should we care?" He sat beside me and pulled me against him, but I resisted

"What's the use, Robert? I'm leaving tomorrow. I don't suppose we'll meet again."

"Give me your address, Tracy. I'll come and see you. Just try to keep me away."

I shook my head violently. "No, you mustn't come. It's no use, Robert. I – I like you, but –"

"Don't talk about love yet, darling. Liking is enough to be going on with."

I had to put him off somehow. I couldn't tell him the truth, so I made something up. I looked at the ring on my hand.

"I know I told you I wasn't really engaged, but – well, if I had my way," I couldn't look him in the eye, "I would be."

"I see." He sounded so like his uncle I looked up. He was sagging with disappointment.

"I'm so sorry, Robert, you're such good company and I've enjoyed every minute I've been with you."

"At least give me your address, Tracy. We could write." I shook my head. "All right, I'll get it from my uncle. I'll get it somehow."

Colin tapped and came in, making a facetious remark about putting "Keep out, kissing in progress" on the door next time.

We sat apart for the rest of the evening. Vivienne joined us and Brett came in with a book which he read until bedtime. Vivienne asked him when he intended leaving for home in the morning. He snapped the book shut and yawned.

"Oh, about mid-morning. We'll lunch on the way again, and arrive home about mid-afternoon."

"Will you have food at your digs, Tracy?" Vivienne asked, "or would you like to take home bread and milk?"

"Thanks, Vivienne, but Dinah will let me have some of hers until I can go shopping."

Brett offered casually, "You can come to us for tea if you like."

"That's very kind of you, Brett," I answered quickly, "but I'll manage. I won't bother Elaine."

"As you like." He threw down his book, said good night and went upstairs.

I followed soon afterwards. I got into bed, but I couldn't settle down. I was restless. Brett's changed attitude puzzled me. I heard the others come up to bed. I turned on my side and tried to remember the words I had flung at him yesterday in the car. In the darkness and the quiet, my own voice shouted mockingly back at me all the things I'd said.

I heard Brett come out of the bathroom and shut his door. It was no use. I got up, found the white quilted dressing-gown Vivienne had lent me and went on to the landing.

Grabbing at my courage with shaking hands, I tapped on Brett's bedroom door. He opened it and stared. He was in his pyjamas and dressing-gown.

"Do you want something?" His cool surprise unnerved me.

"I'm sorry, Brett, but I – can't sleep."

"What do you expect me to do about it?"

"I want to talk to you, Brett. Only a few minutes. . . ."

"All right. Come in."

I went into his room and he closed the door. His hands were deep in his pockets and his shoulders were pushed back stiffly.

"I want to apologise, Brett. I want to tell you I'm deeply sorry for everything I said in the car yesterday. I'm sorry for behaving so badly, too. I'd like to thank you for everything you've done for me, and you've done so much." I traced the pattern on the carpet with my bare toes. "You were right, Brett, to make me drive."

"I know I was, Tracy. Sometimes one has to be cruel to be kind."

"That's all I wanted to say, Brett." I moved towards the door, but he put out his hands and took my face between them. He studied the scar on my forehead.

"It's awful, Brett." My voice cracked. "It's so red and ugly."

"It will fade, Tracy. It will heal up and fade. All scars do. I talk from experience." He stopped and I thought for one crazy moment that he was going to bend his head and kiss it.

But his hands dropped away and slipped into his pockets again.

"Goodnight, Brett."

"Goodnight, Tracy. Sleep well now."

I did.

Robert kissed me good-bye in front of everyone. We were all standing in the hall saying our "thank you's" and shaking hands, when he seized me round the waist. "Good-bye, darling," he said. It was a rather desperate kiss, as though it had been coming to the boil inside him for some time, and I had no chance to ward it off.

The others stared, then discreetly went outside.

"Give me your phone number at least," he said.

"I'm not on the phone."

"The house you live in is, surely?"

"Yes, but we're not allowed calls, not even incoming ones."

He let me go. "I'll contact you somehow. I'm serious, Tracy."

I squeezed his hand and went out to the car. Brett gave me a freezing look and Colin called out, "I'm sitting in the front this time, Miss Johns. Dad told me to."

"I don't mind in the least, Colin," I answered, opening the back door of the car and getting in. "That's your place, beside your father."

Brett gave me another look which came straight out of the Great Ice Age, and I turned away to make myself smile at Vivienne and Robert as they stood side by side, waving us off. I had a feeling Robert would have some explaining to do to his mother.

It was an uneventful journey north. We lunched at the same hotel as we patronised going south. I stayed in the back seat of the car the whole way, and Brett didn't ask me once if I would like to drive. Perversely I was sorry, because now I had got my courage back, I wanted to keep on driving.

When we reached our home town, I was puzzled when Brett passed through the area where I lived and took the road to his own home. I leaned forward. "I told you I wouldn't be staying to tea at your house, Brett. I shall be able to manage —"

"I'm not taking you to tea. I'm taking you to collect my record player. I understood from Robert that you would like to borrow it."

"Oh," I laughed, "that was his idea, not mine."

"There must have been good reason for him to mention it, so I'm lending it to you."

"But I haven't any records."

"You can borrow those, too."

"Oh, but, Brett, I couldn't —"

"Shut up!" he snapped.

I subsided. Why did he keep lending me things and putting me under an obligation to him?

146

We turned into his drive and he and Colin got out. I would have stayed in the car, but he told me to go in. Elaine greeted us on the doorstep and her son, Keith, danced about in the background eager to get at Colin, but Colin dodged him and ran upstairs to his room.

Elaine was, as usual, cool and unruffled. In the hall, Brett asked her, "How are you, my dear? Enjoy your holiday?"

She gazed up at him with her blue eyes and told him the change had done her good. They looked at that moment like two friends meeting, not at all like two lovers greeting each other rapturously after an absence. But perhaps that was how they liked it. They had, after all, both been married before. Perhaps when a man or woman took a second partner in marriage, all the passion and the rapture had been spent on the one who had gone before.

Elaine saw my injury. "Tracy, my dear, what have you done?"

I looked at Brett for a lead. "She had an argument with the windscreen of my car. She knocked herself on it badly."

"You must have done it with some force, my dear." She tutted as she examined it. "Does it hurt?"

"It did, but it's not too bad now. It hurts a bit at night."

Brett looked at me queerly. I couldn't tell him just how much that and other things hurt at night.

"I'll get the record player," he said, and went into his study. "Come in, Tracy."

I followed and stood uncertainly in the middle of the room.

"For goodness' sake, make yourself at home. It might take a few minutes to sort this out. It's years since I touched it."

"Are you fond of music, Brett?"

"I was. I suppose I still am. I don't like listening alone."

"Doesn't Elaine like music?"

"No, she doesn't," he snapped.

The record player was large and heavy and the base was covered in red leathercloth. It looked very smart with its black handle and white lid. He lifted it up to the table, explained how it worked, and showed me how to adjust the controls.

"It's fabulous, Brett."

He pointed to a record holder. "Take your pick."

I slid out the LPs one by one and selected some piano concertos and was delighted to find amongst his collection some recordings of folk music.

"I didn't know you liked this sort of stuff."

He stood beside me and looked at the disc in my hand.

"Why, do you think I'm too ancient? I may be getting on a bit, but I like the message these songs put across. The wish to reshape the world and bring a better life to mankind is not just the prerogative of the young, you know." He smiled for the first time that day.

"Why do you keep saying you're old, Brett? To me, you're not."

He seemed to hold his breath fractionally, then he took the record from my hand. "Sit down. We'll try this out."

We sat side by side and the poignant words of the song brought tears to my eyes. I closed them. I wanted to preserve that moment of shared music for ever.

I felt his hand cover mine, and my pulses throbbed.

"Tracy?" I looked at him. "You cry so easily."

There was a light about his face that made him into a warm and vital human being, and I saw him then as he would be if he were a truly happy man.

He got up when the music stopped and his manner returned to normal. Elaine opened the door and brought in a tray of tea cups and milk.

"That's very thoughtful of you, Elaine. Will you pour?"

We talked over our cups of tea, and I declined Elaine's offer of a meal. I thought it was time I left them together. After all, they hadn't seen each other for over a week.

Brett ran me home and carried the record player up to my room, then left me with a wave of the hand.

What's happened?"

I told her. "Think they did a good job? I got the idea from a magazine. It hides my scar."

"So it does. It might even soften up His Nibs when he sees the new you. You're in hot water with him, Tracy, for not being at the staff meeting."

"I didn't think he'd miss me."

"Miss you? My dear, he nearly had us all scouring the building for you. Then he said not to bother, he'd see you in the morning. So you've got it coming."

"Oh dear. Well, tell me, what happened at the meeting?"

"Plenty. He's really getting things moving now. Amongst other things, he's switching to another examining board, and that'll mean a more modern syllabus for us teachers to follow."

"Is that good?"

"Of course it's good, dreamy. It will bring our teaching schemes more up-to-date. Also," she flipped through her notes, "he received a deputation of sixth-formers and has agreed to re-equip their common room. He's taking the money from the school fund and giving them a couple of new armchairs and table tennis equipment. Also," she turned over a page, "wait for it, he's abolished uniforms for all the sixth forms –"

"*What?*"

"Yes, my dear, and there's more to come – he's abolished the 'house' system, preferring competition between forms instead. And, last but not least, he's done away with the wearing of caps throughout the school."

I reeled backwards. "What will the parents have to say about that?"

"As far as he's concerned, it seems they'll have to get used to the idea. You missed some fun. The older members of staff objected to practically all his decisions, but the younger ones were delighted. Now are you sorry you didn't come?"

Wayne joined us. "Told her about the plans for a new car park?"

"I hadn't got to that yet."

Wayne explained, "He's having the project costed by the county architects, then he'll put the idea to the school governors. He said we might, if we're lucky, get it done under 'minor works'."

"Wow," I said, "he's really getting moving."

"Couldn't be your influence, could it?" Wayne edged closer and his arm went round my waist.

"You've got the wrong impression," I answered coldly. "My influence with him is nil."

"In that case, you'd better have a pretty good excuse if you happen to bump into him today. He ranted about your non-appearance at the meeting." He nuzzled up to my cheek and Jenny withdrew discreetly. "Your hair's nice, Tracy. It suits you. Makes you look a big, big girl." He whispered, "Still engaged to me, Tracy?"

"As far as I'm concerned, we can break it off any time, Wayne."

"End of term, pet. Then I'll set you free. Reluctantly." He put his lips to my cheek.

The staff room door opened. "Miss Johns!"

I pulled away from Wayne and faced the headmaster.

"I want a word with you, please."

I followed him all the way to his study and stood in front of his desk. I braced myself for what was to come. He looked me over quickly and fiddled with the pens on his blotter. "Why were you not at the staff meeting?"

"I'm sorry, Mr. Hardwick, but I'd made an appointment to have my hair done, and it was such short notice, I couldn't alter it."

"I see. Couldn't you at least have sent me a note explaining this? Don't you think it would have been good manners? If I take the trouble to arrange a staff meeting, I expect to get full attendance."

"I'm sorry, I didn't realise it was compulsory. It didn't used to be."

"It is not compulsory." He looked at me. "It is a courtesy I expect from my staff."

"I'm sorry," I said for the third time, "but I didn't intend to be rude. I – I had to have my hair changed to hide the scar. It was getting me down just looking at it so –"

He inspected my new hair-style, but I couldn't tell from his expression whether he approved or not. His tone was softer when he spoke again. "In other words, it was a kind of therapeutic exercise, having your hair done?"

I smiled. "It could be called that."

"In that case, I'll forgive you. But don't let it happen again." I turned to go, but he called me back. "Sit down, Tracy. We have a few moments before assembly." He sat, too, and started doodling symbols on his blotter. "My son tells me your lessons aren't nearly such fun these days."

I frowned. "I must be slipping."

"On the contrary," he smiled, "he says it's because you don't make so many mistakes now."

I laughed, relieved. "It must be those books I borrowed from you helping me to do my homework properly."

"I'm glad you find them useful. Er – you may be interested to know that I've had a letter from my nephew Robert. He asks – no, he insists, that I give him your address. Now what is your view?"

I panicked. "Don't give it to him, Brett."

"Why not? I thought you – liked him."

"Yes, I like him very much," I emphasised "like", "but –"

"For heaven's sake, girl, put the boy out of his misery."

I fiddled with my ring, trying to find the right words.

"Well," he persisted, "does he get your address?"

"No, Brett."

"For crying out loud, why not?"

Why not? How could I tell him why not? I looked at the

ring on my finger. "I'm engaged, Brett."

"Let's get this straight, Tracy, once and for all. Is it genuine, this engagement of yours?"

I crossed my fingers under my handbag. "Yes, Brett."

"Right. Now we all know where we stand. You may go, Miss Johns."

"Brett, I —"

"Yes?" He seemed surprised that I should have any more to say. I turned and went from the room.

CHAPTER IX

WAYNE didn't get the head of department's job. He went to the interview and was furious when a man from another school was appointed over his head.

"I'm doing the work and they turn me down. It was your precious headmaster who shot me down in flames. He asked a lot of loaded questions calculated to throw me." I had never seen Wayne so angry. "Right, from now on, it's strictly non-co-operation from this member of staff," he jabbed at his chest.

"But, Wayne, you had as much chance as the others on the short list. How can you grumble?"

"They didn't have a rotten, sharp-tongued devil stabbing them in the back. I caught sight of the reference he'd written about me, and read it upside down. Unreliable, he said, erratic, teaching methods questionable." He curled his fingers stiffly as if throttling someone, and growled in his throat.

He looked at the time. "Come on, Tracy, it's late. Everyone's gone. I'm going to find a pub, drown my sorrows. Come with me, sweetie, cheer me up."

We passed Brett on the way to the car. Wayne shot him a filthy look and pulled me out of the main entrance behind him. We got into his car and he went down the drive at a frightening speed.

"Calm down, Wayne. You're not safe, driving like that."

We drove around until his favourite pub opened, then he proceeded to drink too much. I began to get worried about him and just before he reached his limits, I persuaded him to take me back to the school to collect my car. I was never so glad before to get behind my own steering wheel. I invited him to my digs for a meal, and to my surprise, he agreed.

By the time we arrived at my place, he had sobered up a little. He swayed as he walked up the stairs and I prayed that Dinah wouldn't come out and see him like that.

As soon as the door was shut, he gripped me and kissed me in a way that frightened me. When I found enough breath to tell him to stop it, he said he was my fiancé after all, and it was time he began to behave like one. I talked him into letting me get some food, and he dropped into the armchair and sat with his hand over his eyes.

We had our meal and finished with strong coffee. His reason returned, but not his good temper. He wandered round and saw the record player on the floor.

"What's this pretty thing?"

I told him. He looked at me slyly. "Well, well, it's got that far, has it?"

I was the angry one now. "You couldn't be more wrong, Wayne."

He lifted the record player on to the table. "Let's have some music, sweetie. You choose."

I picked out my favourite folk song, the one Brett and I had listened to at his house.

"Right," he said, putting it on the turntable. "Sit down, sweetie-pie. Enjoy it."

I was suspicious of his tone, but he sat on the arm of my chair, and I relaxed, closed my eyes, and came under the spell of the music. He stood suddenly, lurched sideways and knocked the table. The stylus skated across the record, making a deep scratch as it went. Wayne reached out and grabbed the playing arm, apparently trying to stop it. He swung it upwards too far and wrenched it clean off the turntable.

I cried out in dismay and he grinned, "Well, well, we've broken golden boy's record player."

"You did it on purpose, Wayne!"

"Did I, sweetie-pie? You can't prove it, can you? I tried

156

to save the record, didn't I?" He was still grinning.

I cried with helplessness and fear.

"Never mind, sweetie. Golden boy won't get angry with you. He's vulnerable where you're concerned, didn't you know? You ought to, the whole staff knows."

I shook my head. "I wish you were right, I only wish you were right."

"Never mind, Uncle Wayne'll try to mend it."

But he couldn't, of course, and he knew it. When he had gone, I stood for a long time staring at the broken playing arm.

I put on my jacket and went out into the evening sunshine to the nearest public callbox. I dialled Brett's number and he answered. A pulse of fear was beating in my throat and I could hardly push the words through my lips.

"Brett, I'm terribly sorry, but your record player's broken."

There was a frightening silence from the other end, so I went on, "Wayne and I were –" but he broke in, "I'm coming to get it." The receiver was slammed down and I replaced the one in my hand. I hurried home and heard his car draw up outside.

My legs were unsteady when I went to the door to answer his knock. He strode across the room, picked up the broken arm, examined it, and put it down. Then he lifted the record from the turntable. He saw the scratch and turned to me, white with anger.

"You've really made a good job of it this time, you and your boy-friend. This was done deliberately and in cold blood."

"It was not, Brett, please believe me. It was an accident. . . ."

He lifted his hand and involuntarily I drew away from him.

"That's all I ever hear from you," he snarled. "An accident. This episode convinces me beyond doubt that you are deliberately setting out to destroy everything I possess. Everything I lend you or give you, you tear apart. My God, you must hate me!"

He took the record between his hands and with a vicious

157

action bent it backwards and forwards until it snapped. Then he threw it into the waste-paper basket.

"From now on you can stay away from me. Keep out of my hair, and keep out of my life!"

He pushed the playing arm into his pocket, closed the lid of the record player and carried it in his arms to the door and down the stairs. Then he drove away.

From that moment, he barely acknowledged me. Whenever we passed each other in the corridor, and it was tormentingly often, he kept his eyes away. If circumstances forced me to speak to him, he was unsmiling and cold. Wayne grew more reckless where our relationship was concerned, both in public and in private. Occasionally, he and Dinah met in my room, but as soon as Wayne appeared, Dinah left us.

I longed for the end of term. At least there was the field trip to look forward to, and although it would be Wayne who was going with me, it would be a relief to escape from the misery of Brett's icy stare.

I gave the boys some special coaching in the work they would be doing while we were wandering in the Pennines. I taught them the general principles of erosion and the effect of weather. We studied the course of rivers and tackled some relevant mapwork. I told them all to buy ordnance survey maps of the area. We traced our route on to large pieces of cardboard, and made sure that all the boys who were coming had one each.

The term straggled to the last day and ended with the tidying-up of registers and the tying up of odds and ends. Wayne came to see me on the last evening of term. Dinah was with me, and as I let Wayne in, she closed the magazine she was reading with elaborate care and lifted herself out of the armchair.

"See you later, Tracy," she yawned. "I can't think why, but I feel the urgent need for some fresh air."

She went to the door, but Wayne got there first. He barred the way. His lips were drawn in to a firm line, his eyes hostile and fixed. I could see he meant business. They confronted each other and the battle began.

"Please let me out," Dinah drawled. "I want to go to my own room. I suddenly prefer my own company."

"That's too bad, *Miss Rowe*, because you're staying right here."

His arms were stretched across the door and Dinah tried to reach round him and grasp the handle. He trapped her hand and wrenched her towards him. She struggled and they moved from the door.

I knew I had to get out fast. I opened the door, pointed madly to the key and hoped Wayne would get the message. He did. I heard the key grate in the lock.

I shut myself in Dinah's room. I felt bored, so I collected her tea things on to a tray, carried them down to the kitchen to wash them. I was drying them when I heard two people come down the stairs, laughing and talking. Seconds later, a car started up and was driven away.

My room felt lonely. The cushion had been thrown out of the armchair, probably to make room for two. I hoped they would be very happy together, and shed a few tears for my own solitary state.

On the first day of the holidays, the boys going on the field trip gathered in the geography room. I inspected their kit and made sure they were wearing the shoes we had advised.

Brett's car was in the drive, and I supposed he had brought Colin to join us. Colin came in at that moment, and I gave him a warm smile. He was the only link I had with Brett these days, and I wondered if he noticed that I never spoke to his father.

I had decided that, as soon as Wayne appeared, I would make him take back the ring. My side of the bargain had been fulfilled. The term was over and there was no need to pretend any more.

I had collected the minibus on my way to school and it stood empty and waiting in the car park. I looked at my watch. Wayne was late. The boys were growing restless. Half an hour passed and still no sign of Wayne. I wondered if he'd overslept or even forgotten. I gave him an hour, then decided to act.

I tapped on the headmaster's door. He came to open it and stared. "What are you doing here? Shouldn't you have left by now?"

"I'm sorry, Mr. Hardwick," I said, in a little girl voice, "but Mr. Eastwood hasn't come. What shall I do?"

He turned quickly and said curtly, "Come in. Shut the door." He lifted the receiver. "What's his phone number?"

I told him. He dialled and waited. Someone answered. Brett said, "Mr. Eastwood? Hardwick here. Miss Johns tells me that you haven't come as arranged to take – what?" He listened, and his eyes narrowed. "I see," he said, looking at me, and listened again. I heard the phone click at the other end and as Brett replaced the receiver, his eyes, which he fixed on me, cut me into little pieces.

"He says, amongst other things, Miss Johns, that he is still in bed, that he intends to remain there and the field trip can go on without him. He also sends you his love with the cryptic message that he hopes you enjoy his substitute. He said you would know what that meant."

I flushed a deep red. I knew well what that meant. I groped for a chair. "What do we do now, Mr. Hardwick? Send the boys home?"

"There's only one thing to do, Miss Johns. *I* shall have to be your fiancé's substitute."

"But, Mr. Hardwick, it will mean breaking into your holiday." He ignored me. He was gathering his possessions and forcing them into his briefcase. "We could send the boys home, couldn't we?"

"No, we could not. Their parents have paid good money for this trip, and they've put them into our care in good faith. We can't let them down." He picked up the phone, dialled and told me to go back to the boys. "I'll join you as soon as I can."

As I closed the door, I heard him say, "Elaine, listen, my dear —"

I stood at the window with the boys clustered round me and watched the headmaster's car roar along the drive to the school gates.

"What's the matter with Dad?" Colin asked, and when I told him his father was coming with us, he groaned.

The others laughed and started getting out of hand. I produced a bag of sweets which I hoped would keep them quiet. In twenty minutes Brett was back, wearing a thick blue windcheater and roll-necked pullover and carrying a large bulging haversack. We loaded up the minibus and the boys scrambled in.

Brett got into the driving seat and I sat beside him. It took some time for the boys to settle down. Their high spirits were only slightly dampened by the fact that the headmaster had come instead of Wayne.

I tried to scale the invisible wall between Brett and myself. "Has it spoilt your holiday plans, Brett, having to come with us at such short notice?"

I took to my side of the wall again when his reply came. "A bit." It was abrupt to the point of rudeness. I wondered if he thought it was impudent of me to use his first name and decided to stick to "Mr. Hardwick" in future.

Brett drove until lunch-time, then we stopped and had our sandwiches in a lay-by. I took over the driving then. I sent him a coded message with my eyes as I strapped myself in with the safety belt. "Do you trust me?" He turned his head away before I could work out the answer.

I drove for many miles northwards along the A1. It was simple, if monotonous, driving, nothing difficult about it. The boys grew bored, then restless, and Brett suggested games for them to play, involving car registration numbers and names of towns we by-passed. Just before we left the A1 at Scotch Corner, Brett took over again. There had been a minimum of conversation between us. We seemed to have nothing to say to each other any more.

The scenery changed now and as we passed through Barnard Castle towards Middleton-in-Teesdale, the landscape grew grand and beautiful. We had been following the course of the River Tees for some time, and now we were amongst the moors in all their brown and sombre grandeur.

It was tea-time when we arrived at Noon Hill House. When we told the boys its name just before we got there, they pretended to shake with fright. "It's haunted," they said, and moaned and clattered their teeth.

"Who told you that rubbish?" the headmaster wanted to know.

"Mr. Eastwood, sir. He said there's a lady ghost who walks about some nights holding her head in her hands. He said he's stayed there before with some boys and he's seen her."

"Damned fool," Brett muttered under his breath, then aloud, "You don't need me to tell you that's the most arrant nonsense I've yet heard, do you?"

"No, sir, but it makes it more exciting thinking it might be true, doesn't it?"

Brett laughed. "Well, all right, but don't start taking it seriously."

They hooted, "Who believes in ghosts these days, sir?"

"Miss Johns, perhaps?" Brett's eyes were maddeningly sarcastic, and I snorted, "Don't be silly." I was glad he couldn't see the niggle of worry at the back of my mind. I wasn't really frightened, but I hoped it was a pleasant, bright house we were staying in, with comfortable beds and plenty of light and doors that locked.

It was, in fact, a large, dark, tumbledown old house. To

say it was derelict would have been an exaggeration, but that was my first impression as we lifted the great iron knocker and waited at the top of the stone steps for the knock to be answered.

I stood back, glad to let Brett take the lead. The heavy front door, holed with woodworm, was opened inch by inch to reveal an elderly lady with a weak questioning smile.

"Mrs. Becking?" She nodded. Brett explained with gentle tact who we were, and she pulled the door wide open for us to tramp in. Her smile widened into a toothy grin as though she were really pleased to see us.

She nodded her head as the bright faces of the boys passed in front of her, and she seemed to have about her the attitude of someone who had waited all day for this to happen. It was good to feel welcome, if not reassured, by the atmosphere we stepped into.

As we tramped up the uncarpeted staircase, the walls threw back the echo of our footsteps. The smell of damp, neglect, and the want of some of the sharp fresh air which abounded outside was overpowering.

There were six bedrooms. The boys were to share three of them, one was allocated to Brett and another to me. Mrs. Becking's bedroom was the smallest of them all.

"Do you live here alone?" Brett asked.

Her north-country accent was not very pronounced. "My sister lives here, too, but she's away visiting." Her voice quavered a little. "I can mash you some tea if you want it."

Brett said the boys were starving, but not to worry, we had brought plenty of food with us. She waved his words away.

"It's ready and waiting. I may be getting on a bit," she turned to me, "but my old hands can still put together the right sort of food to feed hungry mouths, like I did in the old days."

She pointed out the bathroom, which the boys had to inspect one by one, told us to come to the dining-room when we were ready and left us. Then the unpacking began. Brett helped the boys bring in their baggage. I made sure they washed their hands, then I went from room to room unrolling the sleeping bags.

None of the rooms had curtains. Instead there were venetian blinds which looked as though they would fall to pieces if they were touched. I hoped there were curtains in my room, and when I had a spare moment I went along to look. I was disappointed. I tried to close the blinds, but the cord pulled away in my hand.

When I told Brett, he shrugged. "What does it matter?" He walked to the window, stared out. "Nothing but the moors and the hills to watch what you're doing. Not a soul for miles."

"I know, but –" I didn't dare tell him that my nerves had started already.

I looked at the bed. It had an iron frame and a hair mattress. "The bed's not made up, is it?" I said weakly.

"What were you expecting – five-star amenities?" He didn't have to be so nasty, did he? He tried it for softness, and found none. "You'll be all right on that in your sleeping bag."

He dismissed the matter and went out. I wondered what his room was like. I hadn't dared to put my nose in it. In his present mood, I was frightened of what he might say if I did.

We all ate too much tea. There were scones and home-made bread and cakes, fruit pies and large pots of tea. When we congratulated Mrs. Becking, she shook with pleasure. We told her we would get our own breakfasts, but she wouldn't hear of it, so we agreed to let her get them in case we hurt her feelings. She told us we could make up our lunch sandwiches in the kitchen before we left the house each day.

We took the boys for a walk to find the river Tees, and were surprised it was so near. "Can we paddle tomorrow, sir?" asked Miller of the red hair.

"Wait until tomorrow comes, Miller," was the curt answer.

That evening, before the boys went to bed, we planned the route for the next day's walk. "If the weather's fine," Brett decided, poring over my map, which he had borrowed, "we'll try to get to the foot of High Cup Nick. We'll go to Langdon Beck – it's not far – and turn off for Birkdale. Then we'll drive as far as we can, park the minibus and start walking. The footpath's marked on the map. It'll be rough going, but we should make it. You've all got ordnance survey maps?" They nodded. He looked at me. "I'll use yours, Miss Johns." If I thought that meant sharing with him, I was wrong. "You can share Colin's."

I turned away and bit my lip. So he wouldn't even share a map with me. I wandered to the window and looked at the moors through brimming eyes.

His voice called me back. "You're in on this, Miss Johns, aren't you? Or are you opting out already?"

So I went back. I didn't care if he saw my tears. He looked at me queerly, but returned to studying the map.

We settled the boys down in their sleeping bags early because they'd had a long day. My heart beat faster when I wondered what Brett and I would do for the remainder of the evening. I didn't have long to wonder.

In the peace after the chaos of sorting out boys from their pyjamas, towels and soap bags, I wandered round to the back of the house and gazed at the sweeping hills and moorland, now golden in the evening sun. The beauty took my breath away, and I knew that if Brett had been standing by my side, I could have asked for nothing more.

He came round the corner and seemed startled when he saw me. He hesitated, as if undecided whether to turn back or join me, then joined me.

"Lovely evening," I ventured.

He nodded his agreement, stood for a few minutes, hands in pockets, surveying the scene, then muttered, "I'm going for a walk."

He went to the end of the garden and through the gate, leaving me staring at his retreating back with unbelief and misery. Was he punishing me for some unnamed crime? Was this his way of cutting me out of his life? Couldn't he even speak a civil word to me?

I went for a walk in the opposite direction. I didn't see the fells and the wandering sheep, I didn't notice the setting sun sinking from a cloudless sky. I saw only the back of the man I loved going farther and farther from me.

When I returned to the house, there was no sign of Brett, so I went to bed. As I washed in the bathroom, I remembered Mrs. Becking's goodnight words to the boys as they climbed the stairs.

"I expect you've heard about the lady ghost? Well, don't you take any notice. It's no ghost. 'Tis the mice coming out and having fun. They'll do you no harm, boys. Sleep well."

No ghost? Only mice? I shivered, and wished I could share my room with someone. It was late by the time I unrolled my sleeping bag over the mattress. I carried my torch across the room, switched the light off and the torch on. I followed the beam of the torch-light and climbed into the sleeping bag, pulling the pillow into position under my head. I lay still, listening.

Then the fear began. It was primitive in its intensity. I tuned in to the night sounds that hide by day and haunt by night. I heard the bleat of the melancholy sheep, the creaks and the secret whispers, I heard the sound of the silence itself.

I thought I heard a movement, a sighing groan. It's the old lady, I told myself. But I didn't believe it. I grew hot and panicky. My heart was hammering under my ribs. I struggled half-free of the sleeping bag and knew I was in a state of unreasoning terror. That it was self-induced was irrelevant. It was suffocating me and I had to escape from it, find reassurance by touching everyday things.

My mouth was dry, I needed a drink. I groped for my slippers and torch, pulled my anorak over my nightdress and opened the door. Its rusty hinges echoed up and down the long landing. I reached the bathroom, failed to find the light switch, so flashed my torch. No glass, so I used my hand, splashing water between my lips, cold, neutral, reassuring water. I left the bathroom, flashed right and left, trying not to look at the shadows and dark corners. I had almost reached my door when I heard a noise behind me. I felt a hand clamp down on my shoulder and I froze with terror. I opened my mouth to scream, but like a bad dream, nothing came out. A hand was clapped over my mouth and I sagged – not with fright, but with relief. I knew the touch of that hand.

"Brett, oh, Brett," I said, over and over again, covering my face with my hands.

I don't know what I expected him to do, certainly not to adopt his high-handed headmaster's manner and say, in stringent tones,

"Good grief, Miss Johns, pull yourself together."

He followed me into the bedroom and closed the door. He plunged his hands into his pockets and surveyed me coldly. Reaction set in and I began to shake.

"I'm s-sorry, Mr. Hardwick, but I c-couldn't sleep."

The words, so familiar, so evocative of other times, rolled off him. He said, as he had said before, "What do you expect me to do about it?"

"I heard a n-noise. I was s-scared."

"Don't tell me you're afraid of ghosts?" I could hear, even if I couldn't see, his mocking smile.

I couldn't answer because my teeth were chattering. Then I stuttered out a question and knew as soon as I had asked it that my request was outrageous, but I didn't withdraw it. I was beyond the bounds of caring about etiquette and rules. "You c-couldn't st-stay, c-could you, B-Brett?"

There was a moment's incredulous silence, then "*Stay?* Are you in your right mind? Do you realise what you're inviting me to do?"

I turned my head from him helplessly. If he chose to mis-construe my meaning, I couldn't stop him. I suppose I had asked for it.

"I'm s-sorry," I whispered, "to have s-sounded so n-naïve. You can go back to your b-bedroom and really enjoy the joke, c-can't you?"

I could see the faint glint of his eyes in the moonlight that was now flooding into the room, and the large, reassuring shape of him outlined in the semi-darkness. He was so near I would have screamed if he had touched me, screamed with ecstasy, not with pain. I backed away.

"Get into bed, Miss Johns," he snapped, "before I do some-thing I shall regret. Get into bed and stop acting like a child."

A child, he called me? I'd never felt less like a child in my life. I took off my anorak and did as I was told, my teeth still behaving like a machine-gun in full pelt. I curled up in my sleeping bag and adjusted my pillow and lay looking up at him. He stared down at me for a moment, then swung out of the room.

I was late for breakfast next morning. I had taken hours to settle down after Brett had left me, and had awoken sluggish and heavy-eyed. Brett looked at me briefly when I made my appearance half-way through breakfast.

The boys questioned me, "Did you see the ghost last night, Miss Johns?"

I felt too dull-witted to think up a suitable answer, so I just smiled, shook my head and took my place opposite Brett. I tackled my egg without relish. Apart from the fact that it was almost cold, I just wasn't hungry.

"The weather's all right, Miss Johns, so we're going on our walk," Colin told me.

Ken Miller announced that he was taking his camera and there was a chorus of "So am I."

"Have you got yours, Miss Johns?" one of them asked.

"No, I haven't got one now. I did have, but I – broke it."

There was a choking cough from the headmaster's direction and his son banged him on the back. "Have you got your camera, Dad?"

Brett put down his empty cup, and muttered, "Yes."

Colin expansively told the assembled company that he intended taking a picture of Miss Johns, and the others said they would, too.

"Don't waste your film on trivialities," the headmaster growled, and walked away from the table, leaving the triviality in question still eating her breakfast.

We packed two leaning towers of sandwiches, hard-boiled a dozen eggs and filled a dozen flasks. When we set out on the first part of our journey, the sun crept through the low-hanging clouds and illuminated the landscape like a scenic backcloth. We parked on level ground off the road and the boys, released from the restrictions of the minibus, raced up hillocks and rolled down, and hit each other with jackets and maps until the headmaster called them to order. He gathered them in a circle around him to explain the geographical features they should look out for on the walk. He had my map, so I could only stand on the edge of the group listening and watching. It seemed as though he could get on perfectly well without me. "Nobody seems to need me," I thought sulkily, so I wandered off and gazed at the barren beauty of the fells.

It wasn't long before the headmaster called me to heel, like a small dog. He didn't want me near him, yet he wouldn't let me out of his sight. I supposed I'd be more trouble to him lost than tagging along with the rest. Having me around was plainly the lesser of the two evils.

"Miss Johns, take this map and carry on where I left off. I've left something in the bus."

I obeyed ungraciously and when he was out of earshot, I asked the boys what he had been talking about. They tutted loudly at my inattention.

169

"Has he told you about the glaciated valleys you might see?" He had. "What about convex slopes?" They nodded again. "Stepped slopes?" At last I'd found something he had left out.

"Well, I've been through all this in class, but I'll refresh your memories."

At first, as I talked, I didn't notice Brett standing on the edge of the group, listening. When I looked up involuntarily, and caught him watching me, he turned away momentarily confused. When I started talking again, he interrupted me. "That will do for now, Miss Johns. We've come here for practical work, not theory."

I folded the map, threw it down petulantly and walked off in front of the crowd. I knew it was childish, I knew it was setting a bad example, but I just didn't care. Nothing I did was right for him any more.

"Hey, wait for us, Miss Johns!" One or two boys broke away and caught up with him. I heard Colin ask his father why he had gone back.

"To get the first-aid kit, son. Just in case of accidents. They seem to follow me around these days."

Colin burst into raucous laughter. "He means Miss Johns," he shouted to the hills and rocks. "You should hear the things he says about her sometimes."

I turned. I sought Brett's face. It couldn't, it mustn't be true. "Shut up, Colin!" his father roared, and there was something besides anger in his voice, something like desperation, but it was too elusive to define. His face was white with rage, rage at his son, no doubt, who had given the game away. In public, too.

I had felt tired before, but I felt exhausted now. And our walk had scarcely begun. If only Brett would tell me what the crime was that I had committed. It must have been terrible indeed, judging by the way he was treating me. And had I once felt so close to him it was almost as though we had belonged together?

We walked on, and now and then Brett or I would point out some geographical feature to the boys, or bend to search for fossils and other geological specimens. We stopped and admired Cauldron Snout, a great waterfall which hurled itself down two hundred feet in less than half a mile. We searched for gentians, those tiny, pure blue flowers left over from the last Ice Age. We told the boys that these were rare and should be cherished and left alone, as they only flourished in sub-Arctic conditions and would not survive if uprooted and replanted elsewhere.

Some time after that, we stopped for lunch. Around us, hills climbed to nearly two thousand feet. The sun was shining, but even so, the place had a sombre, wild feel about it.

At last we reached our journey's end – High Cup Nick, a great gorge scooped out by glacial action millions of years ago. We sat down again to rest our legs and while Brett talked to the boys about rock formation and glaciated valleys, I lay back and rested my head on my arms. I watched the great billowing clouds moving slowly across the blueness of the sky. I had just managed to squeeze the tension down my body and out of my toes, when Jackson prodded me.

"Mr. Hardwick says will you come and do some teaching, too. He says we came to work, not sleep."

As I raised my aching body upright, I wondered what the headmaster would have done if I had refused to move – made me go to bed without my tea, perhaps?

It was the thought of bed which kept me going all the way back. I lagged behind most of the time. The boys had given me up, and I walked alone. Brett didn't look round once. He was surrounded by the boys and when we reached the minibus, I flopped into the front seat and closed my eyes.

"Miss Johns, will you drive?"

Slowly I lifted my eyelids and looked at him. "What did you say?"

"I said, Will you – Oh, it doesn't matter. Forget it."

I didn't argue, I just rested my head on the side and stared into the distance. I don't remember how I kept going until the boys were in bed. I settled them down and shut myself in my room.

There was nothing else to do, so I went to bed. It wasn't even dark when I slithered down into my sleeping bag. If I could get to sleep before the darkness came, I knew I wouldn't be so unnerved by the noises and the shadows. I was drifting off into a dream when there was a tap at the door.

"Miss Johns," said the voice, "are you in there?"

I didn't answer. "Miss Johns." The door handle rattled and I covered my ears. Someone seemed to be pushing the door, then gave up. I heard Brett's footsteps walk away.

CHAPTER X

I EXPECTED questions next morning, but they didn't come. Not even a questioning look came my way. We prepared the sandwiches again and then Brett put his head in the bonnet of the minibus. I took the boys down to the river and looked for fossils. Brett was so long they got restive and instead of picking up rocks to study, they began to hurl them into the water. Then someone threw a stone at someone else and they all joined in. I tried to stop them. I ran from one to the other taking away the stones, but it was a futile exercise because they only picked up another. I was running between two boys when I felt a stinging pain on my cheek. I cried out and covered the place with both hands. Of course, Brett had to appear at that moment.

"Miss Johns's got hit with a stone!" they shouted, and I wished they'd stop.

I sank on to a boulder and held my face. Brett came up to me and tried to pull my hands away.

"Let me have a look."

I jerked away from him like a bad-tempered child, but he persisted. He prised my hands away. "It's bleeding," he said.

I dabbed at it with a paper tissue. "It doesn't matter. It'll stop. I don't want anything on it."

He took my wrist and started pulling me across to his haversack. The touch of him was enough to make me scream out. I pulled away. "I don't want anything on it!" He must have sensed my near-hysteria and let it go at that.

I realised the boys had been watching us open-mouthed, and I decided that I must be more careful in my dealings with the headmaster for the rest of the week. Colin looked bewildered, and I heard him ask his father later, "Why don't you like Miss Johns any more, Dad?"

I didn't hear the reply. I didn't want to. I started to count the hours to the end of the week.

We took them to the local beauty spots, to High Force and Winch Bridge. We made a detour into Holwick, climbed Holwick Hill, studied the great rocky whinsill cliffs around us, and admired the view. In the afternoon, we went on to Middleton-in-Teesdale and bought fresh supplies of food.

I went to bed early again that night. It was the only way to get away from Brett.

By Wednesday morning it was becoming noticeable that the boys' behaviour was deteriorating. They were noisy and disobedient. They talked and fooled about at bedtime instead of settling down. They had arguments and fights, and Brett spent most of his time keeping them in order. He began to look like a long-suffering parent at the end of his tether. Then it came to me why they were behaving so badly. Like the children in a family with quarrelling parents, they sensed that things were not right between their two leaders, and like such children, they were, deep down, apprehensive and worried. They were rebelling unconsciously against the lack of harmony between us.

Having come to this surprising conclusion, I couldn't tell Brett. I had to keep it to myself. There was nothing I could do to alter the situation. Any overtures of friendliness had to come from him, as headmaster, not me, a lowly member of staff.

That morning the boys had wandered down to the river again. The red-haired boy, Miller, was fighting with Colin. I went between them to part them, and Miller accused me of taking Colin's part.

"He's a creep," he said, "he's the headmaster's son. He's your favourite. He's a baby."

Colin tried to get at him again, but I pushed him back. We were perilously near the river and I tried to edge them away from it.

"Stop it, Rufus," I hissed, "behave yourself."

"My name's not Rufus, *Johnny*," he snarled. At least he had told me my nickname. "Stop calling me Rufus." He nudged me in the ribs, and I overbalanced and went sprawling into the river. It was fast-flowing with the rains that had swept down from the hills and in trying to scramble out, I slipped and went back into the water again. I heard a shouting from the bank and gasped as I tried to get a foothold and make my way to the side. I stumbled over the rocks and grasped two hands stretched out to help me. Those two hands pulled me up out of the water and on to the hard grass-covered earth.

I was gasping for breath, I was soaked to the skin and I was very miserable. "Back to the house," said the voice belonging to the hands. "And a bath." I walked at his side and tripped over a boulder I didn't see through the curtain of my wet hair. Those hands picked me up and carried me and I hadn't an ounce of protest left in my body.

I was dumped in the bathroom, and the taps were turned full on. I heard the old lady's voice outside and a large bath towel was handed in. I knew Brett was still there, so I sat on the chair and waited for him to go.

"Get undressed," he ordered.

"When you've gone," I said.

"Suppose I don't choose to go?" I didn't answer. I just sat. "All right, I'll go for the moment." He went.

I had my bath, got out and wrapped myself in the great soft towel. I stood for a moment enjoying the after-bath warmth inside my body. Then the door opened and Brett walked in.

I stared. "You can't come in here."

"Can't I? Why not?" I thought the answer was only too obvious. He stared down at me with an odd look on his face.

"Perhaps you don't realise how much I know about you already. I told you I helped my sister undress you that day after the accident."

I turned pink and it wasn't entirely from the heat of the bathwater. "That doesn't give you *carte blanche* to come and go in the bathroom when I'm in here."

"Quite right it doesn't. But this is a rescue operation, yet another in my long, long list where you're concerned, so stop being so prudish and dry yourself. If you think I have dishonourable intentions, then think again. We want to get out before it starts raining." I wrapped the towel even more tightly around me and he started rubbing me down with long swift strokes. His hands moved up and down over the towel and I let him do it until I couldn't stand it any longer.

I cried out his name in anguish. He stayed where he was, at my ankles. "I'm sorry, Brett, you'll have to stop," I whispered. He rose slowly and his astonished eyes stared into mine. "I'm not a child, even if you think I am," I whispered again. "Please go."

His expression changed and I wondered if he could see into my throbbing heart. His eyelids drooped and I was mesmerised by him. I felt his hands slide round me, and I was powerless to resist. He was forcing me towards him and I went. My arms loosened their hold on the towel and crept round his neck and as our lips met, the bath towel slipped a little. The kiss went on and on.

As we pulled apart at last, he replaced the towel and wrapped it tightly round my rigid body. I looked into his eyes, seeking love, and recoiled to find only cynicism, and it tore me open like barbed wire. This was not the Brett I knew. His eyes held a look I had never seen before. The insult implicit in them was expressed in the words he spoke.

"If you expect me to apologise, Miss Johns, then you can think again. I'm only human. Having turned down one promising invitation from you earlier this week, I wasn't going to be foolish enough to refuse another."

I whispered, "What are you saying, Brett?" I couldn't believe he was speaking to me.

He went on relentlessly, "What man would say 'no' when given such an unmistakable green light from such an attractive young woman?" His eyebrows lifted sardonically. "Or maybe you mistook me for your fiancé?" He turned at the door and his smile was twisted. "Shall I pass on to you the rest of the message Wayne Eastwood sent you, through me, the day we left the school? He said, 'Tell Miss Johns that I thank her from the bottom of my heart for an unforgettable time last night, and that I couldn't have enjoyed myself more'. He added that he would 'remember what you did for him for a very long time'. End of message. Putting the only construction possible on that statement, it's obvious to me that, where he's concerned, you're only too willing to oblige. I can only conclude that, judging by your behaviour with me this week, it's becoming a habit with you."

I watched him go out. He slammed the door behind him. I felt sick. So now I knew the "crime" I was supposed to have committed! He had believed every word of that deliberately misleading message, as Wayne had intended. I knew that Wayne had been referring to Dinah, but Brett was convinced that it was me.

I knew now exactly what he thought of me. I dressed automatically and combed my hair. I made up my mind. I would leave. Now, at once, I would go. I ignored my conscience when it cried out that I couldn't do it.

I collected my damp clothes from Mrs. Becking. She was surprised and was sorry they weren't dry. Brett caught me in the hall.

"Where are you going?"

"I'm leaving, I'm going home. Now." I tried to keep my voice steady.

He stiffened. "Home?" His surprise turned into cynicism.

177

"Why? Can't you wait to get back to your fiancé?"

I ignored his taunt. "I'm leaving, Brett," I spoke each word clearly, "because after what you said to me in the bathroom, I have no alternative. Your opinion of me is obviously so low that it will be better for us all if I'm out of your way. You've told me before to keep out of your hair. So I'm going."

"That's right," he said bitterly, "use any excuse to escape from your responsibilities. Walk out on me, just like a woman. It's happened to me before, so I'm conditioned to it. Leave me to cope with ten boys just to salve your pride and your vanity."

I stood at the front door, facing out, watching the boys.

"We brought those boys on this field trip," Brett's insistent voice was eating into my determination, "for educational reasons. It's our job as teachers to see that they get as much out of it as we can give them. Our personal feelings and our disagreements should be subordinated to their needs." I wondered when his lecture was going to end. "Even if we do hate each other, our differences should be put aside until we have fulfilled our obligations as their teachers."

So now I knew – he hated me. I turned and looked at him, noticing for the first time the lines around his eyes and an expression in them that I couldn't quite define – was it hopelessness?

He shrugged. "All right, you have my permission to go. This trip you've come on is voluntary, in your holiday period. So you can go back to your boy-friend if he has such a hold over you you can't keep away from him."

He pushed me out of his way and went outside. He told the boys to get into the minibus and I watched as they drove away. I went up the stairs to my bedroom, unpacked the haversack, and returned the damp clothes to Mrs. Becking. She took them with eager hands.

"I'll get them nice and dry for you," she said. "I never did like giving people back damp clothes."

178

I looked out of the kitchen window. "I'm going for a walk," I told her, "a long walk across the fells."

"You're not going alone, my dear?"

"The others have gone to Darlington. I – I didn't want to go. D'you think it'll rain, Mrs. Becking?"

She joined me at the window. "It's certain it'll rain, and when it starts raining in these parts, it goes on raining. Best take a raincoat if you're walking. You'll want some food?"

"I don't need any food."

She insisted. "You can't go without that, my dear. Here, take some milk," she gave me a full bottle, "and some cheese and a bit of bread." I took them to please her.

"No more," I protested. "I'm not hungry."

"But you will be, walking."

So I put the bits and pieces in my haversack, and set off. I had no map, so I had to use my knowledge of geography to guide me. I took the path we had taken on our first day's outing. I knew it linked up eventually with a village called Dufton. I walked and walked; I didn't stop for lunch, I just walked until I reached Cauldron Snout, where I dropped to the ground with tiredness. I drank the milk and lay back and listened to the Tees churning and foaming down the giant steps carved out in the rocks, and which formed the great waterfall.

It started to rain, but I didn't really notice. I began to think. I had to clear my brain and work things out. It was plain that I couldn't go on working at the school. I would look for another job, somewhere in the south of England, as far away as possible from Brett. I got up, stood for a few moments watching the tumbling waters, then I trudged on. I had no idea of the time because my watch had stopped. It must have been late afternoon when I reached Dufton.

In spite of my confused state of mind, I could appreciate its attractions, its red sandstone house round the village green, their gardens tended with loving care.

I found a tea shop and had a cup of tea and a bun, then I

179

started on my walk back to Teesdale. I knew I had many miles to go. I knew I was impossibly tired, but my brain wasn't functioning clearly. It was still raining, a slow, drenching downpour now, which had no mercy on clothes or body. It was persistent and inescapable and it penetrated to my skin. But I didn't really notice.

I was still walking when twilight came, a misty, bleak twilight that soon darkened into blackness. I had no torch, I stumbled, I tripped, but I kept on my feet. I didn't wonder what the others would be doing, I didn't wonder whether I was going in the right direction, I didn't even wonder whether I would ever get back.

My legs were working, my brain wasn't. It was as simple as that. I climbed, then dropped down, only to climb again. My feet were squelching in ground saturated with rain and I wondered idly if I would step into a bog, but I didn't wonder what might happen if I did. I tripped over a rock and fell full length. I didn't bother to get up. I just lay there a long time and dreamed. I dreamed that Brett was with me, that he was holding me and stroking my hair, that he lifted me and kissed me and carried me home.

I struggled back to consciousness and I was alone. I pulled myself up, hoisted my haversack more securely on to my back, and carried on. I had no fear, because I had no feeling. The mist was so thick now I had to feel my way. I started to have waking dreams, visions of warmth and comfort and human contact. I could have sworn I saw someone coming – a group of people laughing and talking. I stared into the blackness, they were so near I put my hand out to touch them, but nothing was there and the illusion receded and died.

I staggered on. I tripped and plunged forward over a body. It moved from under me and I screamed. Then I saw it was a sheep. I lay there, and wished it would come back, so that I could warm myself with its coat and get reassurance from its living, breathing body. I think I slept before I dragged myself

180

up again. I knew instinctively that while I had the strength, I must walk.

I dreamed, as I walked, that I heard a shout, heard my name being called. It sounded hoarse and strange and there were other words I strained to hear.

"*Tracy!*" the voice said, "for God's sake, answer. Tracy!"

I tried to answer, but it wouldn't come. Anyway, it didn't matter, it was only a dream. There was a beam of light and footsteps. I stood and waited for the dream to go. The shape of a man thrust into my vision. He stopped a short distance away.

"Tracy?" The voice made my name into a question, a wondering question.

Again I tried to answer, but nothing happened. I began to crumple up and in my dream he rushed forward and caught me, pressed me to him, said my name again and again.

"My darling," he said, "my own darling. I've been searching for hours. I couldn't find you. I thought you must be dead."

He lifted me and carried me. I didn't try to talk. I didn't want to spoil the dream that took me, after a long, long time, to a house full of boys and noise and lights and a warm, warm bed, with blankets and bottles and sleep, a long, long sleep.

When I opened my eyes, Mrs. Becking was there. She tutted and shook her head. "There's some that don't survive," she said. "But young people, they get away with it, don't they?"

I smiled. "Where's – where are the others, Mrs. Becking?"

"Gone to Alston. It's a right wet day again, so they couldn't go walking. I told them it's one of the highest market towns they'll find in England, so they had to have a look at it."

"It's over a thousand feet up, isn't it, Mrs. Becking?" I asked, just to be conversational.

"Ay, you're right about that. Now, do you want some food? I've had orders from your Mr. Hardwick to feed you, lass. My word, he was in a way last night. He wouldn't leave you, lass.

I said I'd see to you, but he wouldn't let me. He told me he'd rescued you before and knew what to do. Reckon you'll be marrying him soon, lass?" Her eyes were on the ring on my engagement finger. "He won't be waiting long for you, my dear. I could see by the look in his eyes."

I turned away, so that she couldn't see the look in my eyes. She shuffled out to get some food. It was lunch, because I'd woken too late for breakfast. I slept the day away and when I woke again, Brett was there, looking down at me, his face unguarded and full of compassion.

"Brett?" I whispered.

"Hallo, Tracy." He shook his head slowly. "What am I to say to you?"

I could have told him – three little words, that was all he needed to say. But he didn't.

"I'm sorry, Brett, to have been such a nuisance. You – you really must be fed up with me by now."

He walked to the window, stared out. "It's still raining. Mrs. Becking says it'll go on for two or three days." He stood beside my bed again. "What do you say, Tracy – shall we go home tomorrow?"

"Leave a day early? What do the boys think?"

"They agree. They're bored stiff." He walked away again. "You'd see your fiancé all the sooner, wouldn't you?"

I didn't answer. I had to think, I had a problem to work out.

"Unfortunately," he went on, "Jackson's left his haversack in the café we had tea in at Alston. Some clothes and books are in it, otherwise it wouldn't matter. We'll have to go back on our tracks first and collect it, then make our way home. Would you feel fit enough for the journey?"

"Fit enough? Of course." I struggled up, leaned against the pillows. I smiled up at him. "I may be small, but I'm tough. I'm getting up in a few minutes."

"You aren't, you know. You're staying right there. Headmaster's orders."

"Then I shall just have to disobey the headmaster for once. I'm getting up."

The light of battle came into his eyes. He bent down, gripped my shoulders, then immediately removed his hands and slipped them into his pockets. "All right, you win." He turned at the door. "So it's home tomorrow?"

I nodded and he went out. When I joined the crowd later, I seemed to have turned into something of a heroine. They gathered round me, asked me what it felt like to be lost on the moors in the dark, and questioned me so long, Brett had to tell them to stop.

They gave me a present they had bought at Alston – a pendant with a dark red polished stone on a copper base. Colin whispered that his dad had paid for most of it, but the boys had each given something. I thanked them with tears in my eyes.

After they were in bed, Brett and I shared the sitting-room for the first time that week. We didn't speak much. We sat in separate armchairs and looked at magazines. I felt restless. I looked at Brett and saw that he was looking at me. My heart bumped frighteningly, and I got up and walked about the room.

I knew he was watching me. "Looking forward to seeing Wayne Eastwood again?" he asked casually.

"No."

He closed his magazine slowly, put it down, stood up. "What do you mean, 'no'?"

"What I said. No, I'm not looking forward to seeing him again."

We faced each other in front of the settee.

"Wayne and I are not engaged, Brett. We never have been. It wasn't meant to be a genuine engagement. The girl he was referring to in that message was Dinah, not me."

Deliberately, slowly, I pulled off the ring, put it on the

mantelpiece and challenged him, smiling. "I'm giving you the 'green light', Brett."

He looked at me, he looked at the ring, almost as though he couldn't take in what I was saying. Still he stood there, motionless. My heart began to sink. What was wrong? Had I missaid. "And yes, I am in love. With someone else."

"So you're free? You're not in love?"

How was I to answer that? "No, I'm not free, Brett," I said. "And yes, I am in love. With someone else."

He frowned. "I see." He turned away. "Robert's a lucky chap."

Just how stupid could an intelligent man get? "No, it's not Robert!" I shouted, and turned and ran from the room.

He caught me up, pulled me back into the sitting-room, shut the door. His eyes were dazzling mine. "Then by elimination, there can be only one other person. Me."

He gave me no chance to answer. He kissed me and kissed me again. And then he kissed me some more.

I tore my mouth from his. "Brett, please stop. I want to talk to you."

"No talking, Miss Johns. Headmaster's orders. Now be quiet."

"But, Brett. . . ."

"We'll talk to morrow, my darling. Not tonight."

At midnight we parted, and whispered our goodnights on the landing, outside my bedroom door.

"Don't sleep too late in the morning, my love," Brett said, against my ear. "Now I've got you I don't want to let you out of my sight."

I was too excited to sleep, but I must have done, because I woke in the morning refreshed. I was dressed by the time Brett knocked, and he was no sooner in the room than I was in his arms.

"Then it's true," he whispered. "It's real. It did happen."

My kiss proved to him just how real it was. "Shall we tell

184

the boys?" I asked.

"They'll see for themselves even if we don't tell them," he laughed. "This is something we can't keep to ourselves."

We went down to breakfast hand in hand. All the boys were assembled there and they stared open-mouthed, Colin most of all.

"Dad?" he said wonderingly.

His father's arm went round me. "You were right, son, Miss Johns is going to marry me." He took Colin's hand and put it in mine. "Meet your stepmother."

For once Colin had nothing to say.

"But you must stop calling her Miss Johns, Colin, because she's going to be Mrs. Hardwick, and you can hardly call her that, can you?"

The boys laughed, and Colin still stared.

"What will you call me, Colin? Mother?"

Colin came to life. "*Mother?* You're more like a friend."

"My darling," Brett said, "he's just paid you the highest compliment he could pay any woman."

"That's wonderful, Colin. Since I'm your friend, you'd better call me Tracy, hadn't you?"

"Yes, Tracy," he said, and got down to his breakfast.

We said our good-byes to Mrs. Becking and promised her we would go back and visit her one day. We piled into the bus and waved madly as we drove away. It was still raining and the mist hung heavily over the hills, but the boys were as cheerful as if the sun were bursting through the clouds. Whatever had been wrong with their world for the past week had miraculously been put right. Their two leaders had settled their differences and had joined together in complete harmony.

We had our lunch sitting in the minibus in a car park at Alston. We collected the missing haversack and sat drinking coffee and lemonade in the café. The boys crammed their pockets full with biscuits and sweets, and as we bumped over the cobbled streets of Alston and left it behind us, the boys began to sing. Now and then Brett smiled at me and I smiled back at him. We were on our way home.

The going was slow. The road rose at times to close on two thousand feet and at one place went over it. We were enveloped by low-lying cloud which formed a dense, impenetrable mist around us. Our speed had slowed to walking pace. We stopped for tea, still high on the moors, and Brett grew worried about our slow progress. He had driven all they way and was looking tired.

We searched on the map for a youth hostel, but there wasn't one for miles. He thought over the idea of staying at an inn for the night, but we didn't even get that far.

He pulled off the road and turned to me. "It's no good, darling. We'll have to give in. I'm not risking driving through this in the dark. What do you say, Tracy? Shall we stay here?"

I agreed, of course. We settled the boys in their sleeping bags and as they slipped into sleep, sprawled in abandoned attitudes, they looked surprisingly comfortable.

Brett and I climbed into our sleeping bags. He held out his arms and I went into them. I sighed and snuggled up to him. "This is a repeat performance, Brett."

He laughed. "We certainly seem to make a habit of it. This is how it all began for me, my darling, with you just where you are now. I'd never held anyone so warm and responsive as you in my arms before. That night, I fell in love with you. While you were sleeping, I kissed you there," his finger touched my lips, "and when I did it, you murmured my name."

I pulled away slightly to look up at him. "I remember that. I almost woke up, but I heard you tell me to go back to sleep, so I did." I asked him something I had to know. "Brett – Elaine, I thought you were going to marry her. They all said so at school."

"I know they did, Tracy. I knew what they were saying about us. Will you believe me if I tell you that I have never, at any time, had the slightest intention of marrying Elaine?

186

When she first came to work for me, we discussed our positions quite frankly, and agreed that our relationship would remain on an entirely business footing, with no deeper involvement. I think she was secretly relieved and welcomed such an arrangement. And I – secretly – knew that Elaine wouldn't be my cup of tea at all."

"Why, Brett?"

"Because, my darling, by nature she's cold. She's pleasant and good-natured and efficient, but she's cold." His arms tightened round me. "By the time my own marriage ended, I'd had enough of cold wives."

"Brett," again I had to know, "did you love her?"

"Olivia?" He stopped, thought, and went on, "Let's be honest, Tracy – you want me to be?" I nodded against his chest. "She was beautiful and, on the surface, charming. She charmed me, so I desired her, but I don't think I ever loved her." He kissed me gently. "Love, as I now know, is a very different thing." He whispered against my ear that not only did he love me, but he desired me, too. "I've loved you more since I've known you than I ever loved Olivia in the five years we were together, although she bore me my son."

My arms clung to his waist. "Will we have children, Brett?"

"My darling girl, as many as you want." We kissed as we had never kissed before.

"I love you so much, Brett," I whispered as we broke apart.

He whispered urgently, "Marry me soon, sweetheart."

As soon as he liked, I told him. "We'll contact your mother. Will she want to be there?" I said, probably, I didn't know. He kissed me again when I said that. "My sister will come."

"What about Robert?" I asked. "What will he say about us, Brett?"

"Ah, now, Robert. Shall I tell you what I wrote and told him? That he didn't stand a chance with you, and that if you ever decided you didn't want Wayne Eastwood, then I intended to take over where he left off."

187

"Poor Robert. What did he say to that?"

"That his mother had told him something similar, that he didn't think there'd been any harm in trying and that he wished me all the luck in the world."

"But how did Vivienne know?"

"My darling, I'd written and told her all about you. That's why I wanted you to come south with me at half-term. I wanted to introduce my sister to the girl I loved."

"So you loved me then?"

"I told you, sweetheart, I've loved you a long time."

"Brett, will you ever forgive me for breaking so many of your possessions?"

He lifted my hair and put his lips to the scar on my forehead. He lifted my right hand and kissed the scar on my palm.

"You've always been there when something's gone wrong, Brett."

"My darling, I'm quite reconciled to the fact that I shall have to spend the rest of my life rescuing my left-handed, accident-prone wife from all kinds of unimaginable nightmares. But," he lowered his voice even more, "that will make her even more precious to me."

"Brett," I persisted, "suppose I break a lot more of your things?" I frowned at his profile in the darkness. "You know, you're taking an awful risk, marrying me."

"I'd be taking an even greater risk if I didn't, sweetheart," he laughed. "It's not safe to let you out of my sight!" He became serious. "From now on, Tracy, everything I possess is yours to break. But one thing you must promise never to break. This."

He took my hand and put it over his heart. I answered that to his complete satisfaction.

"When we wake up in the morning," he said, pulling me even closer, "the mist will have gone and the sun will be shining. You can sleep soundly, my love, because from now on, I shall always be around to pick up the pieces!"

THIS MOMENT IN TIME

Lilian Peake

Lynne Hewlett was young and eager and full of modern, advanced theories where her job was concerned. Christopher York, unfortunately, made it quite clear that he utterly disagreed with them – and he was in a position to put a stop to them any time he wanted, to the detriment of Lynne and her career. He was opinionated and narrow-minded and – hateful! she thought. But all this didn't stop her falling in love with him – disastrously, as it turned out, for not only did he obviously dislike her intensely, but he was equally obviously interested only in his old and dear friend, the beautiful singer Angela Castella.

A GIRL ALONE

Lilian Peake

Sparks had flown between Lorraine Ferrers and Alan Darby from the moment they met – and it was all Lorraine's fault. She was, it had to be admitted, inclined to be opinionated and prejudiced – and one of her deepest prejudices were against journalists, of which Alan happened to be one! But Lorraine was so busy trying to hate him that she entirely failed to realise that she had in fact fallen in love with him instead. But hadn't she left it a little late? After all the bitter words she had flung at him, how could Alan do anything but dislike her? Was it any wonder that he so obviously preferred the possessive, ultra-feminine Margot French?

Coming in April

MAN OF GRANITE

Lilian Peake

It was ten years now since the end of Kathryn's brief, youthful marriage to Jon Wright. They had parted in anger and misunderstanding, and she had never seen him again. Since then, the only important thing in Kathryn's life was security. It was for security that she was now on the verge of marrying Francis Rutland, a man old enough to be her father, for whom she had nothing but a kindly regard. It was hardly the moment for Jon to come back into her life again, and in circumstances which meant she would be seeing him every day. Still less was there any future in her realising that she loved him as much as she ever had – since he made it quite clear that she now meant less than nothing to him.